SECRET SANTA

A Cold War Christmas Tale

David Holman

Rapier Books

SECRET SANTA – A Cold War Christmas Tale
Paperback Edition

© David Holman 2024

David Holman has asserted his rights under the Copyright, Design and Patents Act, 1988, to be identified as the author of this work. All rights reserved. No part of this publication may be reproduced, stored in a retrieval system, or transmitted in any form or by any means, electronic, mechanical, photocopying, recording, or otherwise, without prior written permission from the Publishers.

This book is a work of fiction. Names, characters, businesses and organisations as well as places and events are either the product of the author's imagination or are used fictitiously. Any resemblance to actual persons, living or dead, events or locales is entirely coincidental.

ISBN 9 798 34418 0 755

Cover design by Delta Designs © 2024

First published in 2023 by Rapier Books

Also by the author

Alex Swan Mystery Novels

Flames of Thunder

Wings of Death

Countdown to Terror

Island of Fear

Spears of Defiance

Tracks of Betrayal

Hayes & Homewood Thrillers

Fallen Shadows

For my family

Waiting

Nikita Metzinov sat nervously inside a small supply room looking at his watch. He had only twenty minutes left to freedom, but had he made a big mistake?

Outside in the exhibition hall of the National Museum of American History, the sea of dinner suits and evening dresses of Washington DC's international diplomatic community held their half-filled glasses, exercising flirty smiles and seductively snaking arms. Some of them were probably wondering how the next remaining few hours of this Christmas gala will progress, infused by the anticipation of what might happen afterwards. Above their heads, the flags of all the nations present draped down, bringing a cascade of colour and a sense of national pride to the patrons. The exhibition hall also contained galleries displaying artefacts of American history ranging from the paintings to the pottery.

Nikita knew it would not be long. He also knew the ever-present KGB would most probably be searching for him right now. The distraction of Santa's arrival had been enough for him to make his disappearance, but it had all happened so fast. It was only four days ago, he had announced his intentions to defect. The Americans had organised themselves for it. He had wanted this more than anything - to be free of the regime the current US President had dubbed, *The Evil Empire.* Back home in Moscow, the Soviet Union's military attaché to Washington DC had no one; his brother was dead; his mother and father as good as dead. America offered everything he could not have in his own country. In America, he could say what he felt like saying without repercussions. Of course, he would have to tread carefully, keep the low profile as the FBI had suggested— away from the opportunities of silenced pistols or discreet syringes loaded with deadly toxins. The FBI were more than aware of the illegals – the scattered, highly-trained KGB sleeper agents working within the USA. Despite the heavy security, surrounding who were seen as traitors to the motherland, these men and women had managed to get to a number of defectors, some being targeted for on-the-spot assassination, while others were kidnapped to face prosecution back in Moscow, where they would be shaken until the last granule of useful information had spilled out onto the cold stone floor deep in the catacombs of the Lubyanka. There were two options. They would either be turned as triple agents or dragged out to the courtyard, put against the scarlet-splattered wall and shot.

Up to now, Nikita had no knowledge in what the Americans had planned for him. Would he stay at a safe house somewhere in Washington DC, or would he be whisked away across the States to some remote location, away from prying eyes and retribution for his betrayal? One thing he did know, is he had successfully delivered his gift to them. The Americans would be pleased. This act also showed the seriousness of his decision to claim political asylum in their country.

He looked at his watch again, it had only been five minutes since he had been hastily ushered into this room. The door had been locked behind him by the grey-suited female FBI agent escorting him. His mind started to race, what would Davinski, the KGB Rezident be doing? Nikita imagined the panic on his face right now, as he ordered his two men, Kirov and Tutinev to search the floors of the museum, then having to sheepishly inform the ambassador his military attaché had possibly defected to the West. The horror on the ambassador's face would be followed by a recall back to Moscow to face questions from the politburo. It would mean he would not be able to return to Washington and the lavish lifestyle and privileges that come with being an overseas representative of the party. For a few days now, Nikita had suspected that Davinski had become suspicious. The frequent social meetings with a man who was seen as his American counterpart in the Pentagon, Jack Ramsey, had become a surveillance nightmare. It had been Ramsey who had magically paved the way for Nikita's wish to come true. The American had set the wheels in motion.

As he surveyed the small room with the shelves filled with cleaning products, there was someone else on his mind — someone who over the last few days had entered his heart. She would also be out there, desperately looking for him. For the brief moment they had been together this evening, they had parted badly. It was a stupid argument. He knew why she was angry and had tried to explain, but her rage and despair of not seeing him again had been too much for her; she had walked away, and it had been too late; Santa had arrived, and this had been his cue. He started to think about her, wondering if she would be safe. Kirov would have informed Davinski about their relationship and whirlwind romance after following them through the park. Had he now put her life in jeopardy? How easy would it be for Davinski to break her? As the minutes clicked away, he could not stop himself worrying about Irina. It would be a double blow for his ambassador – first the news of losing one of his attachés to the Americans, then the shock his own secretary had aided his escape.

Outside, he suddenly heard the creak of a door open - the one he had been pushed through earlier by Jack Ramsey. He could now hear heavy footsteps approaching. Suddenly, there was a knock at the door, the coded three taps. A man's voice then recited the memorable password Ramsey had given him. This was it. Walking over to unlock it, Nikita began to think back to all the events which had led to this moment. Although it felt like a lot more, it had only been days ago since he had uttered those magic words to Ramsey. Now, it was time. With the Christmas gala still in full swing, it was time for Nikita Metzinov's very own Christmas miracle.

The Walk-In

It was six days ago that Nikita was invited to have dinner at the Ramsey's home to meet the rest of the Ramsey family.

Jack Ramsey introduced him. 'Nikita, this is my wife, Barbara, and these are my kids, Luke and Sarah.'

Nikita noticed the children had been excited when their father had informed them, he was Russian and worked at their embassy.

'It is indeed an honour to have me in your home, Mrs Ramsey,' he smiled.

Jack Ramsey took his greatcoat and hung it on the hook next to those of the rest of the family.

'Come through, make yourself at home,' beckoned Mrs Ramsey. 'Jack tells me you both do the same job, only you do it for *your* country.'

Nikita nodded. 'That is correct.'

Luke rushed forward. 'I have a big collection of model airplanes, and a few of your Russian ones. Do you wanna see them?'

They both looked over at Luke's father who nodded his approval.

'Please, I would be most honoured,' smiled Nikita.

Luke led the Russian upstairs to his room.

The boy pointed up to a silver painted twin-engined plane with red stars on the wings. 'This is a Beagle bomber.'

Nikita smiled. 'Its proper name is an Illyushin IL-28. Only NATO call it the Beagle.'

Luke beamed. 'Wow. I didn't know that.'

'We still have quite a few still flying.'

Luke pointed to a smaller model jet. It was also painted silver. 'This is a Mig.'

'A Mig 15 to be exact,' added Nikita. 'This was Russia's first jet fighter plane.' A grey-painted jet model suddenly caught his eye. 'You have the MIG-25.'

Luke smiled. 'Yeah, the Foxbat. Dad got it for me on his last trip to Japan. He told me he's seen a real one, too.'

Nikita smiled. He knew exactly what the boy had meant. He took a few moments to admire the rest of Luke's collection hanging from fishing line on the ceiling. 'It is a fine collection,' he commented. 'In Russia we have other models of our aircraft. In my last position in Moscow, I was responsible to see that the toy makers would not be giving away any secrets when making their products. I will see if I can get some sent to the embassy for you.'

Luke beamed again. 'Gee, that would be cool!'

Jack Ramsey entered the room.

'Dad, Nikita's going to get me some more Russian airplane models.'

Ramsey smiled. 'That's great to hear, son.' He turned to his Russian guest. 'Thanks, Nikita. Now, it's time for dinner, guys.'

Later that evening, over cigars and a glass of bourbon in Ramsey's study, his Russian guest suddenly felt more relaxed.

'That was an excellent meal. Your wife is a very good cook.'

Jack gave a chuckle. 'It was only chicken. You need to be here when she bakes her pies. Now they're really something.'

Nikita smiled, then took a sip of his bourbon. As he allowed the flavours to melt on his tongue, he decided it was just enough liquid courage to deliver his bombshell. 'I have become so disillusioned with my country, Jack. The hardliners in power just want to keep us in the past like they were in the days of Stalin. I have had enough of this. All I want is peace between our two countries. Their paranoia leads straight to accusations. I talk of the Korean airliner incident in September. The military budget has been increased to meet the Politburo's demands for new weaponry. Operation Ryan has caused madness amongst them. The SALT treaty is a joke. It is all one-sided and has been for years,' raged Nikita. 'Rrazryadka, what you call Detente, the most hopeful avenue for peace, is now over because of this foolish invasion of Afghanistan. We are just what your president called us, Jack - an evil empire.' He suddenly felt good in finally telling someone else what he had been bottling up inside him like a keg of gunpowder.

Noticing the anxiety on the face of his Soviet friend, Ramsey probed further. 'What are you trying to tell me, Nikita?'

After a slight hesitation, the Russian continued. 'I have lost my brother to this unjust war in Afghanistan. My father is in a Siberian labour camp after being arrested for protesting the war. My mother is also in a labour camp outside Moscow for joining his anti-war campaign.'

'Jeez. 'I'm so sorry to hear this, Nikita.'

Nikita paused, then after taking a breath knew it was time, time to reveal his true intentions. 'What I am saying to you, Jack, my friend, is, I am done with my country. What are my chances of claiming political asylum here in America?'

Ramsey's jaw dropped. 'You do know what you're saying?'

Nikita nodded slowly. '

Ramsey shook his head. 'Jesus, you're goddamned serious about this, aren't you?'

Nikita nodded again. 'I am, Jack, very serious.'

Ramsey shook his head. 'You realise how dangerous this is, especially with someone in your position? You're chaperoned everywhere by the KGB.'

'I am willing to take the risk, Jack. Believe me, I have thought of nothing else. I would go right now if I could.'

Ramsey paused to think. 'Let's not be too hasty. This is big, real big. It's gonna need planning, thinking through.' He gestured to the window. 'Your KGB man is outside. I'm hoping he hasn't got one of those long-range microphones in the car right now.' Ramsey turned back to his guest. 'You know what your people could do to your parents if you defect?'

'They are already dead to me, Jack. Even in my position, I have not been allowed to visit them. I feel that if I do this, I will in some way honour them for their sacrifice.'

Ramsey sat down. He was still in deep thought.

'Will it be possible for me to defect, Jack?' Nikita was now becoming insistent for an answer.

Ramsey looked up at him. 'I can't see a problem in you being given asylum, Nikita. The problem is how the hell are we going get you to us? I need to make a call. I know someone who may be able to help you.' He walked out of the room leaving the Russian to his thoughts.

Nikita took another slug of bourbon. He had made his move. It was now up to the Americans. Would they accept his offer, or would they see this as some sort of KGB sting?

In the hallway, Ramsey picked up the receiver and dialed a familiar number. His call was answered in four rings. 'Bob. It's Jack. You're not going believe this, buddy, but I think we have a walk-in—direct from the Soviet embassy.'
Ramsey returned to the study and sat down to see the Russian was now pacing the room. Nikita noticed Ramsey's face had changed. It now looked more business-like.

'I just spoke with a contact in the FBI,' said Ramsey, he's coming over right now. He wants to talk to you.'

Nikita went to the window. 'What about Kirov, outside? He will see him.'

Ramsey picked up his cigar. 'Relax. He's coming in through the back. I'll just go and tell Barbara to let him in. Bob's a family friend. We can trust him. He looked down at his near empty glass. 'I think we could both do with another drink.'

Twenty minutes later, Ramsey introduced Bob Donahue. The FBI agent looked sternly at the Russian then reached into his briefcase and took out what looked like a walkie-talkie. 'Hold up your arms. I need to check you're not wired.'

Nikita complied, allowing Donahue to switch on the device. It gave out a continuous bleep as it was swept around him. Donahue then gave a satisfying nod to Ramsey. 'He's clean.' The FBI agent pulled a chair and sat down facing them both. 'I'm on the Soviet Desk. We spend most of our time tracking illegals. Sleepers, we call them. There's a lot of your spies over here, probably been here quite a while. Maybe even pretending to be good 'ol American citizens with legitimate jobs and families. Jack has told me you want to seek asylum.'

Nikita nodded. 'That is correct, Mr Donahue.'

'You know what this all means? You can never see your country again, your family, your friends—your girlfriend.'

Ramsey quickly informed Donahue about Nikita's family.

'I do not have a girlfriend,' Nikita added.

Donahue nodded. 'I understand.' He climbed out of the chair. 'Well, you do seem to have your reasons. You do realise even if we manage to pull this off, you'll have to spend some time being debriefed? I'm talking about having to undergo a series of lie detector tests.'

Nikita stared at him, candidly. 'I am willing to do what is necessary, Mr Donahue. Please tell me what you wish me to do.'

The agent smiled. 'Please call me, Bob. I'll have to take this back to my chiefs. They're going to want something in return.'

'I'm only sorry it will not be another MIG 25.'

The two men laughed at the Russian's sheepish remark in reference to his friend from his days at the Moscow Air Academy and how seven years ago he had defected to the West in his MIG 25 FOXBAT jet fighter by landing it at a Japanese airport and claiming asylum in the United States. He glanced over at Ramsey. 'You were there in Japan when Belenko landed it at the airport? Your son told me.'

Ramsey just nodded. 'I flew out there the next day.'

Donahue quickly butted in. Although the aircraft had eventually been shipped back to the Russians, there were still a lot of secrets regarding the September 1976 incident. 'You're the Soviet Air Attaché. I'm sure they'll think of something.'

Nikita nodded his appreciation. 'So, what is to happen now?'

'We'll need to keep in contact with you. Jack will be in touch. We need a few days to make the arrangements. I suggest you meet Jack in the park. Do you know where the statue is down by the river?

'Yes. We usually meet there.'

'Jack will meet you there two days from now at 11:30am. Let's keep it in the daylight so it just looks like a lunchtime casual meeting. Now listen carefully to this. You will offer Jack a cigarette, but you will have forgotten to bring your lighter. When you search for it, that will be the signal that you still want to go through with this. Jack will light the cigarettes in view of your

KGB tail. You'll both stand looking out on the Potomac. Jack will instruct you on what to do next. Do you have all that?'

Nikita nodded. 'Yes. I fully understand.'

'I have something for you,' said Donahue, reaching into his jacket pocket. He handed him a small metal box.

'What is this?'

'Why don't you open it and find out.'

Nikita opened the box and pulled out the smallest camera he had ever seen.

'Call it a *Welcome to the US* present,' said Donahue.

This was it, Nikita thought. They wanted something. 'What is it you wish me to photograph?'

'I'm sure we'll think of something. Just keep it safe for now.' He pulled out another camera, this time a Nikon compact from a shoulder bag. 'I need to take your picture for our files.'

Nikita tucked the small box into his jacket, then stood against the door to allow Donahue to take his photograph.

Donahue then shook his hand. 'Good. You'll hear from us soon, Mr Metzinov. Jack and I now need to talk.'

Nikita nodded curtly. 'Of course. I will bid you a good evening, gentlemen.'

Ramsey called the rest of his family to the front door. It would look better this way for his Soviet friend's minder. He opened the door and had him shaking hands with everyone. Nikita then gave Barbara Ramsey a kiss on both cheeks in the Russian custom. It was all in full view of a very bored Alexei Kirov slumped in the driver seat of the embassy car. On hearing the farewells from the Ramsey family, the little Georgian jolted to an upright position and yawned, before starting the car. Nikita climbed into the back and gave him a sharp nod in the mirror.

Ramsey watched the car and waved as it drove away from the house. He then went back inside, poured two more glasses of bourbon then went back upstairs to his study.

'This is big time, Jack,' announced Donahue, taking the glass. 'If we can pull this off, it'll be a major coup for us.' He thought of what the Russian had mentioned earlier. 'This is even better than Belenko and his FOXBAT at Hakodate Airport. Can you imagine what he could give us?'

Ramsey suddenly had a thought. 'His position would give him access to aircraft technical manuals, wouldn't it?'

'Sure, it would. What do you have in mind?'

'There's one Soviet airplane we don't know much about. And it's one we need to.'

'Go on.'

'The Tupolev TU-160. NATO have given it the codename, Blackjack. It's supposed to be a similar design to our B-1, only bigger. Right now, we don't have much intel on it. If Metzinov could get us the technical specs, it'll put us in a good position to compare it with the B-1. All the hype about it, may turn out to be just like what we discovered with Belenko's Mig. Then again, if it *does* turn out to be major threat, we can work on something to countermand it.',

Donahue took another sip of bourbon. 'Do you think you could persuade him to hand it to us?'

Ramsey nodded. 'I think I could - in exchange for his freedom. You saw how desperate he is to come over to us.'

'Absolutely,' smiled Donahue. 'The problem is going to be getting him out. He's chaperoned everywhere he goes in the city by the KGB. He makes any move to defect; they'll sure know about it.' Donahue paused for a few moments. 'Yeah, that could be a problem. We'll have to think of something so that he loses his tail.'

'Any ideas, Bob?'

'Donahue paused. 'I need to think. I'll be in touch after I've talked this over with my chief.' Donahue grinned. 'I can't wait to see his face in the morning, when I tell him what we have.'

Santa Yuri

Bob Donahue sat patiently opposite his department chief, Mike Farnham as he read his report. When he had finished, Farnham looked Donahue in the eye. 'Is this for real, Bob?'

'He disclosed his intentions just last night. He's ready to come over to us.'

'And you checked him over?'

Donahue nodded. 'Used the new equipment. He was as clean as the dinner plates in the White House dish room.'

Farnham shook his head. 'How the hell are we going to pull this off?'

'I'm working on it. Something will come up, but we've gotta act fast. An opportunity like this sure doesn't come along too often.'

Farnham read another section of the report again. 'So, what is this, Blackjack?'

'It's the Russkies latest supersonic bomber airplane. Jack Ramsey has a few grainy photos of the prototype, but it seems to be a doppelgänger for our B-1. I mean, what he showed me, it's as if someone actually stole the plans from Rockwell's.'

'And you think Metzinov will play ball and give us this, Blackjack.'

'I think he will, Mike. Metzinov is their military attaché. If he says he can get us the technical specs on her. I really think he'll deliver. All we have to do is come up with a foolproof plan to bring him home.'

Farnham shook his head again. 'This is incredible. I'm taking this to the Secretary. She's not going to believe it.' He looked at his watch. 'Darn! It'll have to be later. She'll be busy choosing a dress for the Diplomats Christmas Gala on Friday night. Jesus, I don't envy her wardrobe advisers right now.'

Donahue laughed. 'Well, you know her better than anyone, Mike. You're the one who's been married to her for almost twenty years.'

'All of them good, Bob, except when she's shopping for Goddammed dresses,' added Farnham.

Donahue laughed again.

'I suggest you get back to your team and get your heads together,' said Farnham. 'Make this Priority One!'

Donahue finished his coffee and walked towards the door. 'Thanks, Mike.'

'No, Bob. *Thank you*, and Jack Ramsey. Just keep me up to speed. Let me know what you come up with to get our boy.'

Donahue gave him a mock salute. 'Will do.'

'And Bob?'

'Yes, Mike?'

Farnham smiled. 'If Metzinov doesn't come up with this manual, we can always send Clint Eastwood over to steal the airplane.'

Donahue chuckled, recalling last year's *Firefox* movie.

'I'll keep that in mind.'

After getting himself another cup of coffee, Donahue met with his team and briefed them on the Russian's walk-in. He looked across at one of the men. Steve Kember had been with him for two years after graduating from MIT.

Donahue handed each one of them a copy of the photograph he had taken at Ramsey's house. 'This is our walk-in, Nikita Metzinov, military attaché in the Soviet embassy.'

'Question is, how we going to get him?' asked Kember, studying the face of the Russian.

'That's what we're doing right now.' replied Donahue. 'Let's have some ideas. He's chaperoned everywhere by the embassy's KGB minders. It's not gonna be easy. Their Rezident, Davinski, is a slimy son of a bitch from the old school. I've read his diplomatic file. And according to some intel I already got from our man, he said his minders are both ex-Spetznatz. So, guys. I need your input on this. How do we get one of their top men over to us when he's being watched twenty-four seven by Soviet special forces guys?' Donahue shuffled some papers then looked across the table at the three men. Along with Kember, there was Harry Fennan, an old veteran from the Hoover days and Joe Gimble, another recent recruit, this time from Berkeley. 'Let's get onto this, use your contacts and let's see some action. We'll reconvene later, at 1600.'

Donahue returned to his office to find his secretary, Linda Grierson waiting for him. She had rested a box full of old Christmas decorations on his desk.

Donahue shot her an irritated glance. 'Not now, Linda.' Ignoring his dismissive remark, she reached into the box and pulled out one of the items - it was a Santa in the form of a Russian doll. 'As always, Santa Yuri starts with you, Bob.' She placed it on his desk. The object had become a tradition on the Bureau's Soviet Desk. Each of the staff would unravel the sections of the doll and place a personal message inside wishing the team a happy holiday. Santa Yuri had been named after the current Soviet premier and someone had drawn a pair of glasses around the eyes to give it more of a resemblance. Inside it all the other pieces had had the same treatment. To Linda Grierson's annoyance, no-one had ever owned up to doing it. As soon as everyone had contributed, Yuri Santa would be placed under the office Christmas tree until the annual party when she would read out the messages, despite how crude some would turn out to be. 'Be sure to pass it round once you've put your message inside.' It wasn't a suggestion from his secretary, it was more like a command. She had been with the Soviet Desk for seven years and since then no file had been misfiled, no litter had been left on the desks and if anyone who had tried to pass on a task, they could do themselves, would warrant that person having to buy her lunch.

As she sailed out of the door with a stack of files for Archives, Donahue sat back in his chair and sighed. He had to come up with something and fast. The meetings with Ramsey in the park were always chaperoned. He was also aware of the leaps in surveillance technology the Russians were introducing. If they did manage to aquire these long-range microphones, it could make things more difficult. He finished his coffee then looked over at the Santa doll. Might as well get this over with, he thought. There was one Christmas when he had passed it to another desk and had completely forgot to put in his message. Grierson had decided he had to buy her lunch for a week at a restaurant of her choice.

Not wanting to see a heavy tab from the *Old Ebbitt Grill* again, he reached for it then as he began to unscrew it, suddenly remembered how stiff the first shell was to open. She had showed him many times, but he still couldn't quite remember the technique. Without it, it would take some effort to prise it open. He sat with it in his hands and stared at the smiling bespectacled face. Over the far side of his office, sat a photograph of the actual Soviet leader himself shaking hands at the start of the disastrous 1979 second stage of the Strategic Arms Limitation Talks. It was when he was still head of the KGB.

Donahue suddenly remembered what Ramsey had told him about Metzinov's outburst regarding SALT, then concentrated on the doll again, this time taking in the red Santa suit and bushy white beard. Suddenly, his eyes flicked once again to the photograph then back to the doll, which he had now managed to prise open to reveal a slightly smaller identical Santa inside. For a few seconds he sat gazing at it then glancing back at the photograph, smiled gleefully. 'Son of a bitch! He started to laugh, then shook his head. 'Son of a bitch,' he said, again.

Bob Donahue shot out of his chair, and still holding the red Russian Santa doll, threw open his office door. 'Steve, Harry, go and find Joe and get your asses in here.' He held up the doll. 'I think I've found a way to get our man out.'

Fennan spied the object in his hands. 'Is that Santa Yuri?'

Donahue nodded. 'It sure is, Harry. And he's gonna help us get our boy.' He sat down, placed the doll on the table then unscrewed it to reveal the smaller one again.

'See?'

Fennan looked over at the others. It was a

questionable look that asked if their chief had maybe snapped his cap.'

***

In the early afternoon, Jack Ramsey acknowledged Donahue from a bench behind the Capitol building. Donahue had called him to meet with him urgently. When he had told Ramsey he thought he had found a way to get Metzinov out, Ramsey had rushed over from the Pentagon.

The dome cast its shadow over them as they shook hands. On the way, Ramsey realised he had not yet eaten and although he was now almost halfway through a baloney salad club sandwich, realised it was too much to eat. He offered the other half to Donahue who declined with a wave of his hand and sat down beside him in view of the Capitol Reflecting Pool. 'So, what's the good news, Bob? You said you've found a way for our boy.'

'We have a plan, Jack. The Christmas Diplomats Gala at the Smithsonian on Friday evening.'

'The one your wife is hosting. You're thinking he'll be able to come over during the party?'

'It's probably going to be our best shot.'

'The KGB will be there. They'll be watching their embassy staff like hawks.'

'I'm aware of that. So, we got to come up with something to distract them.' Donahue smiled. He was suddenly lost in his own thoughts. Ramsey gave a puzzled expression. 'What is it?'

Donahue smiled again. This time it was a lot broader.

'It's Christmas, Jack, and what we have in mind, may just work.' He reached into his overcoat and pulled out the doll.

'Ramsey suddenly had an even more puzzled expression on his face. 'What the hell is that?'

'Meet Santa Yuri, Jack.'

Ramsey stared down at the doll, shaking his head. 'Santa Yuri?' Suddenly he could see the resemblance to the Soviet leader made clear by the spectacles. 'Santa Yuri, he nodded. 'I still don't get you, Bob. What's the doll got to do with getting Metzinov over to us?'

Donahue patted Ramsey on the shoulder. 'Do you still believe in Santa Claus, Jack?'

'Why the hell do ya ask me that?'

'Cos he's gonna help us with your boy, Jack. We're gonna take Metzinov right under the noses of the KGB.'

Ramsey was still confused. He stared back at the doll. 'If you say so, Bob.'

'Just trust me, Jack. I'm confident this will work.'

Ramsey still looked blankly at him. 'Okay. I still don't get you, buddy, but it sure sounds like you gotta plan.'

'We sure have, Jack.' Donahue rose from the bench.

'One you're not going to believe. And it's all down to Santa Yuri, here.' He unscrewed it again and Ramsey gazed at the identical smaller one inside then shot his friend a blank look.

'How?'

Donahue turned and looked down at him. 'You'll see,' he said, with a smug grin, putting the doll together again then back into his overcoat. 'All we have to do, is hope Metzinov believes in Santa Claus.'

Blackjack

A few days later, Nikita checked his watch then walked out of his office. On the desk was his silver lighter. It had been a gift from his parents for his twenty-first birthday. At that moment, he began to think of them. Even with all the special privileges that came with his position in the party, he had still been forbidden to visit them. He then started to remember his younger brother's funeral his parents had not even been allowed to attend despite being held at his local church in Gorky.

Earlier, Nikita had met with Davinski and informed him of his meeting with Jack Ramsey. This was the general procedure and would prompt the KGB Rezidentura to arrange for a security detail.

Metzinov walked towards the exit acknowledging Irina Statinova, the ambassador's secretary on his way out. He always enjoyed talking with her and whenever the opportunity arose, they would have coffee together in the embassy canteen. During these interludes, they would casually flirt with each other and talk about other embassy staff. He felt she admired his company as much as he admired hers. 'It is such a beautiful day for this time of year, Irina,' he commented, smiling.

She looked him directly in the eyes and smiled back at him. 'Are you going out, Nikita Yuriesevich?'

'I have to do my usual casual walk in the park with my counterpart at the Pentagon, Irina.' He gave her a sly smirk. 'I have some more useless information for him.'

Irina laughed. 'You are a bad man, Nikita Yuriesevich.'

'Do not worry, Irina. It is never one-sided. Jack Ramsey gives me plenty of worthless rubbish in return. It is a little game we both play.' He nodded to his appointed KGB minder who would be following him through the park. This time it was the tall Ukrainian, Sergei Tutinev.

He turned back to Irina. 'Perhaps, I will see you later. We can have coffee together in the canteen.'

Irina gazed deeply into his eyes. 'That would be very nice.'

Nikita smiled at her. 'Later, then.' He then turned to see Tutinev standing only a few steps behind him, giving him a mischievous grin through his rugged looks.

Nikita ignored him and allowed him to follow him out of the embassy building.

Ten minutes later, he spied Ramsey standing by the Martin Luther King memorial. He was feeding the ducks in the basin with the crust from a chicken and mayo sandwich his wife had prepared for him before he left the house this morning. The American acknowledged him and waved. They then walked towards the John Erricson memorial.

Ramsey knew not to say too much about the other night, especially with Tutinev trailing a few metres behind them. He led Metzinov over to the riverwalk and they stood leaning against the low wall, looking out at the Arlington Memorial Bridge.

Nikita offered Ramsey a Russian cigarette. Ramsey took one from the packet, but to Tutinev, the pretence of scrambling around his coat for his lighter, assumed he had accidentally forgotten it.

Nikita apologised to his American opposition with a sheepish grin, and Ramsey laughed then lit their cigarettes. The signal had been received. Nikita had confirmed his request for political asylum in the United States. Ramsey also knew the Russian was not wired. Nikita was also aware that now he was to defect, he would be asked to provide something valuable for the Americans. With all walk-ins, there had to be some kind of offer in return as a test. He had access to many sensitive documents and files. *What would they ask him for? How would the small camera Donahue had given him be put to use?*

Ramsey discreetly checked the distance was safe from the KGB minder.

As an extra precaution, a young man and woman stood a short distance away admiring the same view. Inside the woman's handbag, was an electronic jammer device to prevent any possible long-range microphone activity.

With the counter-surveillance tradecraft in place, it had not taken long for Ramsey to get to the point. He glanced over at the couple.

The man gave him a discreet nod. Ramsey turned back to the Potomac their backs to Tutinev. Nikita's American friend was well aware some KGB operatives had been trained to lip-read. 'It's now safe to talk. I'll get straight to the point. We need the technical manual for the TU-160 - what we have codenamed: BLACKJACK. Can you get it?

Nikita gave a hard swallow. He suddenly thought this request impossible. His duties were actually a far cry from the Soviet Union's latest strike bomber. They mostly involved evaluating the warplanes of NATO. All his work at the moment was centred on the new Tornado now equipping European air forces and weighing it up against their own SU-24 — an aircraft with a similar role. He was also heavily involved with the US Navy's new F-18 tests. How could he take himself away from this to suddenly concentrate on the TU-160 instead without raising suspicion? 'This will not be easy,' he replied eventually. 'My duties do not involve me with the TU-160. If I was to show a sudden need to research it, it might raise some suspicion. Is there anything else you need, something I may be in a better position to provide you with?'

Ramsey sighed. 'In a few days, two of our B-1 bombers are flying over to Fairford. England, to carry out some low-level trials in Scotland. This was going to be kept all low-key, but Bob Donahue thinks it would be better that everyone knows about it. The Pentagon are releasing a press statement later today. This should give you an excuse to get your hands on the technical manual for the TU-160, considering its similarities to our airplane.'

Nikita considered this. 'The B-1 aircraft in Europe will certainly raise an alarm with Moscow. I also do not think the technical manual is in our Washington archives. I will have to request it to be sent in the next diplomatic case.'

Ramsey studied a rowing boat with four occupants as they glided past them down the river. 'The camera Donahue gave you. Is it safe?'

'Yes. I have hidden it well in the office.'

'That's good. Use it to take photos of the pages. Donahue also informed me how we're going to get you out.'

'How is this to happen?'

'I don't know much, yet, but it's this Friday, the Diplomats Christmas Gala at the American History Museum. You'll be coming over to us on the night.'

Nikita screwed his face. 'How? The KGB will also be there.'

'We already know they will. Donahue has come up with something that should work. Believe or not, Nikita, according to him, you'll be walking out right under their noses- and they'll never know.' '

Nikita's eyes widened. 'And how will this happen?'

Ramsey smiled. 'Bob said that all you have to do, Nikita, is believe in Santa Claus.'

Nikita turned to the American. 'I do not understand your meaning of this.'

'Don't worry. I don't really understand it myself. Bob wouldn't tell me. I suppose it will all come clear on the night. Just deliver the film you'll take of the technical manual.' Ramsey then grabbed the Russian's arm, pulling him closer to the rail. Behind them, Tutinev sat on a bench looking bored.

Down below, the surf of the Potomac crept up onto the shingle. Ramsey tapped the rail. 'Reach your fingers under here. You should feel a hole. I need you to use the little box Bob gave you to put any messages into it then place it deep inside. You must also try and leave your work around 7pm from now on until Friday. There will be an FBI agent observing you each time, just in case you need to make contact using the box. They'll also be watching your tail. Don't worry. These guys are pros at tradecraft. You'll never know they're there.'

Nikita sighed. There was more to consider. The Americans wanted this instruction book. There was no doubt he wanted to defect, but how far was he prepared to go to gain his freedom? He knew his superiors were already suspicious of him; the acquisition of the minders when he was out and about in the city had been the latest sign his increasing friendship with a top US official at the Pentagon was becoming a cause for concern. Not only had he to find a way to get his hands on the manual, but he would also have to find a way to try and shake off his shadow when the time came to deliver it. This plan to get him across to the Americans started to sound like a fairytale. *Why should he be asked to believe in Santa Claus? What was all this about? Had this American, Donahue, suddenly gone insane?* 'I trust you, Jack. But I need to know more of this plan. We haven't much time.'

'Don't worry. As soon as I know what Bob is up to, I'll let you know.' They shook hands in sight of Tutinev. 'I'll be in touch,' said Ramsey.

***

The next morning, Nikita was presented with a stroke of luck. A report had crossed his desk regarding the deployment of the B-1 to Europe. The strategy of the Pentagon's press release had worked fast. He now had his chance. He looked at his watch. He had ten minutes before his meeting with the ambassador.

His morning meeting had begun in the usual way. On the long mahogany table, tea and lemon would be served alongside a shot of Vodka. Micha Detrev had only been in the top job in Washington a few months. He looked across at his military attaché over black-framed spectacles.

'You have seen the reports from Moscow referring to the B-1 deployment to the United Kingdom?'

'Yes, comrade ambassador. But having worked on the Tornado evaluations and now the F-18, I am somewhat vague as to the specifics of this aircraft.' This was it, he thought and decided to make his move. 'What I do understand, it is not too dissimilar to our TU-160 prototype.

'What NATO have now codenamed: Blackjack?'

Nikita nodded. 'In fact, I would go on to say that it is almost a carbon copy, only ours is bigger and I think superior in comparison.' Nikita hoped his ambassador would appreciate his admirable comments, and as Detrev smiled thinly at this, Nikita decided to play the ace card. 'I do not believe we have the technical manual for our aircraft in our embassy archives, comrade ambassador. It would be good for me to compare performance data with the American aircraft as part of my evaluation report.'

The ambassador nodded in agreement. 'Very well, I will contact Moscow and arrange for one to be placed in the next diplomatic bag.' Nikita tried not to show too much enthusiasm. 'That would be most useful, comrade ambassador.'

Detrev leant back in his chair. 'Your friendship with Jack Ramsey.'

Nikita was suddenly awestruck. 'What of it, comrade ambassador?'

The ambassador raised a reassuring hand. 'Don't worry, it is good. I was thinking we could use this to our advantage. Perhaps to obtain more information on these B-1 deployments.'

'I very much doubt we would get what we needed, comrade ambassador. I am already dubious of the amount of disinformation I get from Mr Ramsey.' Nikita smirked. 'Naturally, I have given plenty in return after liaison with comrade Davinski.'

The ambassador let out a guttural laugh. It seemed his shot of vodka was now beginning to take effect. 'The meddlesome KGB have an answer for everything.'

Nikita smiled. 'Indeed, comrade ambassador. However, I feel that the Americans may become reluctant to continue with these mutual exchanges because of Davinski's men I have accompanying me.'

The ambassador paused to consider this. 'I will speak to Davinski about this. We cannot scare Ramsey off. This mutual exchange, however trivial is still good for us. Perhaps we could put one of our domestic comrades onto him, find out if he has any vices we could manipulate. A man like this could be useful to us. Perhaps a chance liaison with one of our swallows, may well aid this manipulation. Believe me, I have met with some of them. I'm sure Ramsey could easily be tempted,' winked Detrev.

Nikita shook his head. 'I very much doubt this, comrade ambassador. Jack Ramsey is happily married. He has a family. I have met them.'

'Yes, you went to dinner at their house, I am told.'

'Indeed, I did, comrade ambassador. It gave me another opportunity to increase our friendship. Who knows what we could gain from this.' Nikita gave a smirk. 'Perhaps a future invitation to visit the Pentagon?'

Detrev laughed again. 'This indeed would be a great achievement, comrade.' He sifted through a set of documents and pulled out a letter. Nikita recognised the Smithsonian letterhead. 'I have an invitation to attend the Christmas Diplomatic Gala event, and as well as my good wife, Katya, my secretary and my KGB contingent of course, I also get to bring along my attachés. He stared Nikita in the eye. 'I think it would be good for us to attend, despite what has happened to our two nations this year. Who knows? Your friendship with Jack Ramsey may open doors to new relationships and opportunities.'

Nikita smiled. 'I would be most honoured, comrade ambassador.'

Detrev reached into his desk drawer and pulled out a small bottle of vodka. Nikita watched as he poured himself out another shot. 'As far as a gift is concerned,

I have ordered a set of special stamps commemorating our link-up with the Americans in the Apollo-Soyuz mission.'

Nikita nodded. 'A fine gift, comrade ambassador.'

Detrev gulped down his second shot of the morning. 'I thought perhaps a return to the good days of our comradeship with the Americans would remind them we can one day all be friends again. Perhaps sometime in the future, and despite our political differences, we will see an international space station, jointly manned by astronauts and cosmonauts, or maybe travel to the moon together.'

'That would indeed be a great moment, comrade ambassador.'

As Nikita left the office, he smiled to himself again. The technical manual would be arriving the next morning, and with this invitation to the Christmas Gala confirmed, he would be in an ideal position to carry out his intentions. He was suddenly now excited about how this was going to play out. Entering his office, he checked his hiding place he had chosen for the camera. Pulling out the book from the shelf, it was still there. He then thought of what Ramsey had said. It had played on his mind since their meeting. *Why did Ramsey want him to believe in Santa Claus?*

The Drop

Nikita arrived at his desk the next morning to find the usual black pouch for his attention, all the correspondence sent via the diplomatic bag from Moscow.

After pouring himself some coffee delivered earlier by Irina, he set to work removing the plastic seal and examined the contents. He pulled out a black file and smiled as he read the silver leaf Cyrillic label on the front cover with a 3-view drawing of the TU-160. Stamped across it in permanent red ink was the word: *Confidential* in Cyrillic script. He flipped over the cover and stared warmly at the production drawings of the four-engine supersonic bomber that preceded the technical data on this new aircraft. He noticed each page of the file was bound in place by a set of wire coils.

Nikita nodded in appreciation. It would be easy to flip each page over when taking the required photographs. There were now other things to consider. Obtaining the manual had been the easy part. He now had to make contact with Ramsey and organise his move. If his KGB minders were still accompanying him, this would not be so easy. His next scheduled official meeting with the American was to be tomorrow. Hopefully, Ramsey would know more about his defection and what Santa Claus had to do with it.

He reached across his desk and picked up the gala invitation which had also been delivered by Irina. It was in two days' time. His window would be far too tight. He had to get out a message before then to let them know he had the manual. Could he use the dead drop mentioned by Ramsey, the one in the park by the memorial? Nikita also knew how resourceful the KGB could be. Perhaps they were already familiar to this dead drop site? If they were, then planting his message would be the end of him. His diplomatic apartment was the other side of the park. He would normally be driven to it. This evening, he would fancy a walk.

Outside somewhere, Ramsey had promised there would be an FBI agent. The Americans were more than aware how valuable he was to them. They would do what they could to protect their latest asset. As long as he left to go home at 7pm as instructed - there would be someone there to watch over him. He could still make the drop.

***

After a rigorous day compiling the comparison report, Nikita filed away the TU-160 technical manual, put on his coat and walked out of the embassy.

As he exited through the gates, he spied Irina in her black Ushenka hat and doing up her coat. The sun had long gone down and the colder night was creeping in over the capital.

Nikita caught up with her. 'Irina, wait I walk with you.' She stood holding her collapsed umbrella. The forecast was it was expected to rain later. 'Are you walking through the park?'

Irina nodded. 'Yes, Nikita Yurisevich. Are you also walking through the park?'

Nikita smiled. 'That is good,' said the secretary. 'Sometimes it can be quite frightening for me. There are sometimes American boys standing around and although I do my best to ignore them, they come over to me and start to ask me awkward questions. I get scared and sometimes I feel like this for the rest of the evening.'

Nikita gave her a reassuring smile. 'Then it is good I walk with you tonight. You should have told me this before. He stopped in front of her, and noticing her scarf was not hugging her neck, he was suddenly compelled to gently tighten it for her. 'I will always walk with you now. If this is okay.'

Irina gave an elated smile. She had also felt something when he had adjusted her scarf. 'Of course, Nikita Yurisevich. I now feel safe by your side.'

Nikita suddenly felt a lump in his throat. He had never felt for this woman this way before, but tonight he could sense something else about her. The warm glow in her eyes at his offer to protect her after his spontaneous move with the scarf had sparked something inside him. He turned to walk out of the embassy gates and saw she had taken up station by his side. He looked around the streets. There were other people walking, some young couples strolling along in a romantic embrace, a group of youths sharing a joke, but he couldn't see anyone he would identify as a possible US FBI agent.

Nikita walked alongside the girl, his hands in the pockets of his overcoat. In the right pocket was the small box. He needed to get to the rail overlooking the river. With Irina by his side, this would look far better than executing the maneuver alone. All he had to do was guide Irina to it and pause for a cigarette while leaning against it to take in the view of the river. There, having already extracted the box, he would carefully move his hand to push the box inside the recess. Ramsey had emphasised that he must press the box into place so that it doesn't fall out and drop into the river, or even worse, when the tide is out, onto the shingle for anyone to notice it.

Nikita decided he must try to drop his message. There was only two ways out to the other side of the park. One was alongside the river; the other was over the bridge. At this time of night, the bridge was not safe. It had over the years become a haunt for drug users and drunks. Everyone seemed to be walking towards the river which would help in what he was about to do. He had suddenly found his excuse.

Coming to the statue he turned to her. Let's walk down the path along the river.'

Irina suddenly snaked her arm around his for security. 'I was hoping you would suggest this, Nikita Yurisevich. I love looking out at the water. The way the city lights twinkle off it, so reminds me so much of walking by the Moskva.'

Nikita smiled at her and suddenly felt an unusual tingle as the crook of their elbows snaked around each other. He then suddenly heard footsteps behind him. He turned his head to see Kirov. He was keeping pace at a strategic distance from them. Could he still do the drop?

Behind Kirov was another man walking a small dog in the same direction. Nikita noticed he had cut his pace in line with the KGB shadow. Was this his FBI agent? He turned to look forward again and felt Irina clasp tighter around his arm.

Is everything alright?' she asked.

Nikita smiled. 'Yes, Irina. Please do not worry. It is procedure for all attachés to have a KGB escort when in a foreign country. It is for my own protection. Which means you will also be protected while we are together.' He looked back at Kirov again and gave him a friendly nod which was met by a curt one in return.

A few minutes later, they had reached the riverwalk. Nikita stopped. 'I need a cigarette.'

The woman unhooked her arm allowing him to access his right coat pocket.

Nikita pulled out his packet of Russian cigarettes sent over in the diplomatic bag. He extracted one and lit it. He offered the packet to Irina who put up her mittened hand. 'I do not smoke.'

'Then you are much healthier than I am, Irina.'

They both laughed. Nikita then noticed Kirov had stopped to sit down on a bench. He too was now enjoying the same brand of cigarette.

Behind him, the man had stopped to allow his dog to sniff at a tree. Nikita moved Irina towards the rail, discreetly checking he was still in line with the memorial. At the rail he rested his arms, taking more of his cigarette. He now needed a distraction. 'It is a beautiful city, Irina. We are very fortunate to be sent here to represent the Motherland.'

As she looked across the Potomac in response to his comment, he slowly placed his hand on the slab and hooked his fingers under it to feel for the recess. In a few seconds he felt it. The box was in his left hand. He moved to meet the other hand then passing the box under the right hand, moved his fingers over the ledge and pushed the box inside the recess. While doing this, his fear of being seen by Kirov had got the better of him and his feelings for the woman standing next to him were accidentally revealed. 'It is nice being with you tonight, Irina.' He looked into her face beneath her furry hat and smiled.

'I am also thinking it is nice to be with you tonight, Nikita Yuriesevich.'

They locked eyes on each other, slowly moving their heads closer to each other until their lips touched.

Nikita had not anticipated this. His intentions were to use her to make the drop look more natural. Now, those times when he had looked at her at the embassy, imagining what it would be like to hold her in his arms or caress her naked body in his bed, had suddenly become possible. All this time she had felt the same way and he had never known it until tonight.

She moved closer to him nestling into his side. 'It is getting cold. Shall we walk now?'

Nikita patted her. 'Of course.'

They walked on and suddenly had a thousand things they wanted to say to each other. Their conversation was now limitless. Irina spoke of her family back in Leningrad. Nikita spoke of his in the Gorky region of Moscow. Then, as they neared the exit to the park, came the more personal questions regarding their love lives past and present.

'So, you have no one waiting for you back home?' Nikita asked.

Irina shook her head with sadness in her eyes. 'My fiancé was killed in Afghanistan. I have no one else. What about you? Do you perhaps have a girl waiting for your return from overseas duty?'

Nikita shook his head. 'I think my work has always got in the way of finding love, Irina. But my brother was also killed in this damned and pointless war. He decided not to tell her what had happened to his parents.

They had walked on further. Kirov was still behind them, but Nikita noticed the man and his dog had not exited the park. Had his message been picked up?' They arrived at a set of apartment blocks.

'This is where I live,' said Irina.

'I am just a few streets further down this road.'

They stood looking at each other a few moments. *What was to happen next?*

'You could come in. We could watch television together', Irina had finally said. 'I have a moussaka in the fridge.'

Nikita smiled. 'I am not one for watching American sitcoms or their propagandist news programmes, Irina,' he lied. 'But will you have dinner with me tomorrow evening?'

Irina nodded. 'Yes, Nikita Yuresevich. I will that very much.' They moved close and kissed again.

'I will see you tomorrow, Irina. Thank you for a nice evening.'

Irina let out a small laugh. 'We have only walked home together, Nikita Yuresevich.'

Nikita kept a straight face. The look he gave her was one of sincerity. 'But I have still very much enjoyed being with you, even if it was just a walk home.' They kissed again. 'Goodnight, Irina.'

'Goodnight.'

He watched as she turned and walked up the steps to her apartment block.

Further down the road, he started to recall this series of unforeseen events. He hoped the drop had been a success. He was sure he would hear from Ramsey very soon, but what he had not expected was Irina. He suddenly began to feel different regarding what he was about to do. With what happened with them tonight, he saw his life had suddenly changed.

Espionage

The next day, Nikita caught Irina in the canteen at breakfast. The ambassador had insisted all his staff have an hour in the morning to be in what he had expressed as 'fully fueled' for the day. He was desperate to talk to her, but she had been dragged to another table by her other embassy clerical staff colleagues.

She glanced over, met his eyes and smiled.

Nikita saw Davinski had walked in. He had caught their exchange.

'Good morning, comrade Metzinov.

Nikita nodded curtly. 'Comrade Davinski'

'You are looking forward to the gala on Friday night?'

Davinski nodded. 'Yes. Very much.'

Nikita looked over at Irina again. She shot him another smile.'

Davinski also turned to look at her. 'Yes, comrade. It should be a good party, especially for you, I think.'

Nikita forced a grin and watched him walk over to help himself to coffee from the machine.

Later, Irina entered the Military Attaché office with some papers and placed them on Nikita's desk.

'We are still okay for dinner, this evening? he asked.

She nodded. 'Where are we going?'

'I will book a table at a beautiful Italian restaurant I have been going to with the American, Jack Ramsey.' He looked at her inquisitively. 'You do like Italian food?'

'Of course. She checked behind her, she had closed his door, and leaning over the desk gave him a quick kiss on his cheek. She then smiled at him teasingly. 'Until this evening, Nikita Yuresevich.'

He watched as she turned on her heels and glided out of the door. Suddenly, his cascading dilemma soon came flooding back. He shook his head, then checking his watch, walked over to the door. Opening it, he peered out into the corridor. To his left, he had just caught a last glimpse of Irina as she disappeared through a set of double doors to descend the stairs back to the ambassador's office. To the right, it was clear. This was now the perfect time to take the photographs.

Moving back to his desk, he opened the drawer, pulled out the manual, and after placing it down, noticed the sun glare on the document. He reached behind him and closed the blind. The glare had been removed, but now it was too dark to take the photographs. The Americans would struggle in making out the drawings and photographs of the plane. Cursing to himself, he switched on the desk lamp and no matter how much he adjusted the angles, he found the light hindered his intentions. This could only be a one-time opportunity – a rapid act of espionage. What was he to do now?

Outside the window, the light was beginning to fade, and on the horizon, dark clouds were beginning to draw nearer. Nikita remembered the weather report had forecast heavy rain for the rest of the day with a slim chance it could turn to snow. He began to think of his evening and how he would be huddled with Irina under her umbrella as they walked to the restaurant in the lashing rain. He then wondered if Kirov or Tutinev, whoever it was to be the tail for this evening, would also be carrying an umbrella when they followed them. Also, if they left around 7pm, there would be another person following them for a while. He suddenly had an image of three umbrellas in a convoy and sniggered to himself.

His thoughts then returned to the manual. The light was getting worse. He sighed. realising he would have to postpone the task. His message to Donahue stated he had received the manual and would deliver the film tonight. It would now have to be tomorrow. This would leave him only one more day to take the photographs before the Christmas Diplomatic Gala.

As he placed the manual back into the drawer, he began to feel his stomach churning again. His feelings for Irina were growing stronger. *What would happen after dinner? Would it be back to her place or back to his, or would he decide not to put her through the heartbreak, and for her sake, insist to her they just remain work colleagues?* There was also something else that just occurred to him. What he was about to do on Friday could put her in danger. It would not take long for Davinski, having witnessed what had occurred in the canteen, to discover their feelings for each other and more so, assume she had played a part in his defection. She would then be arrested and on the first Aeroflot flight back to Moscow, and on arrival, who knows what fate would await her? Defection is seen as treachery to the Motherland

and therefore punishable by death. *Was he prepared to sacrifice her in exchange for his freedom?* Then there was his surprise all set for her this evening. Over dinner he would present the tickets to tomorrow night's ballet at the Kennedy Centre. He had been lucky to obtain them through another embassy colleague who unfortunately had a sudden engagement and was unable to attend. The chasm Nikita knew he was already in - had just got deeper. He would be meeting Ramsey soon. The promise was to hand over the film. Now he would be meeting him empty-handed. *Would Ramsey see this as a failure, that he was unable to provide the Americans with what they wanted from him? Also, would this now have an impact on the defection?*

He flicked through the manual. Also on his desk was the press release for the Rockwell B-1A deployments. The first thing that struck him was the uncanny similarities of the two aircraft. The design profiles were almost identical, suggesting a clever act of espionage. Nikita was already aware that the TU-160 was bigger in comparison to its American counterpart. And, also to him, and without bias, felt his country's new supersonic bomber looked more streamlined. However, he also knew that just like the MIG-25, appearances were not everything.

Underneath the menacing looking facade, lay a spaghetti of problematic systems that were years out of date. It had been one of the things he had had to put a brave face to when involved with the sales of Soviet war machines to other countries' military forces. Selling to Warsaw Pact contemporaries was never difficult, but when the Kremlin had decided to spread their sphere of influence into the oil-rich countries of the Middle East and North Africa, it had been harder to convince the skeptical Arab and African nations to buy Russian in favour of American. Nikita had always admired some of the American aircraft designs — the nimble General Dynamics F-16 lightweight fighter being a perfect example of versatile engineering. He had not been surprised the plane had now equipped most NATO countries as well as the air forces of Pakistan and Israel. Russia was still looking to rival it and Nikita had been heavily involved with the programme before shifting over to evaluate the other great threat to the European theatre - the Panavia Tornado. In a state of war, these low-level strike bombers would take off from their bases in the United Kingdom, West Germany and Italy to deliver a devastating blow to the Warsaw Pact. There was also the interceptor variant under development for the British to replace their ageing American

Phantoms. From the intelligence gathered about its radar capabilities, this could make the penetration of their airspace by the USSR's long range reconnaissance force far more of a challenge.

He looked at his watch. It was time to meet with Ramsey again and there was much he had to say to him. He closed the manual, and as he placed it in a safe behind him, hoped tomorrow's weather would be on his side.

***

Ramsey was again standing, throwing bread crust at the ducks swimming in the basin. As much as he tried to feed one particular bird, the others had ganged up on it and took the morsels before it could get to them. He looked up to see Nikita approaching followed by his KGB minder. Familiar with the proceedings, Kirov sat down on the usual bench and took out his cigarettes.

'Good afternoon, Jack,' greeted Nikita.

They walked towards the statue. Ramsey had noticed a look of disappointment on the face of his Soviet counterpart.

'I'm afraid I was unable to take the photographs. The light in the office was poor today. I will try again tomorrow.'

'No problem,' said Ramsey kindly.

Nikita let out a relieved sigh. 'I was worried you may have thought I did not want to go through with it. He handed him a carrier bag which Kirov had checked and cleared the contents before leaving the embassy. 'These are for Luke. I had them sent in the diplomatic bag, like I promised to him.'

Ramsey peered inside and pulled out the two model kits of Soviet jet fighters. 'Wow, Nikita. These are excellent. The SU-7, and I've always admired the MIG-21. Luke's gonna love these. Thanks.'

They had reached the riverwalk and turned to view the Potomac.

'I have faith in you, Nikita,' said Ramsey. 'I know you're not playing us. All is arranged as we discussed. You just need to be ready.'

'I will be. I promise, Jack. I am still curious what you said that I have to believe in Santa Claus.'

They started walking again. 'All I know is that at some time in the evening, Santa is going to be making an appearance. He's going to bring the gifts for the ambassadors. How this all fits with you coming over, to us, sure beats the hell out of me. We've just got to trust Bob knows what he's doing.'

'I'm sure Mr Donahue knows what he is doing. My life will be in his hands.'

Ramsey halted. 'This is it, buddy. Next time I see you will be at the museum, on Friday.'

They shook hands in full view. 'See you at the museum, Jack.'

Lovestruck

Irina tightly clutched Nikita's hand as they walked quickly through the beating rain and into the restaurant in Downtown.

Behind them was Tutinev. Rather than expose himself to the adverse weather, he had opted to drive in the embassy's Ford surveillance vehicle. When they had left the embassy, Nikita had seen a man waiting at the bus stop across the road - the Americans were still watching over their impending prize.

After watching Metzinov and the girl walking the few blocks, The FBI agent had decided there was not to be a dead drop message at the memorial tonight and had hailed a taxi. He would go home and give Donahue a call.

The Maître de showed them to a table situated in the centre of the restaurant. The table was adorned with a red and chequered tablecloth with a wine bottle candle holder in the middle. Italian folk music was being piped from hidden speakers. A waiter soon came to them and presented them each with the wine list.

'It is so nice, here,' Irina commented. She looked around at the other patrons. The place was almost full. She knew that Nikita had chosen well.

The waiter soon returned for them to order their wine. Nikita chose a dry chianti in agreement with Irina. The waiter then presented them both with the menu while he fetched their wine. They had ordered a starter of antipasti and ciabatta rolls.

Irina leaned across the table. 'Do you miss Moscow, Nikita Yuresevich?'

Nikita helped himself to another piece of warm ciabatta, breaking off a piece and dipping it in a saucer of olive oil. 'I certainly do not miss the food.' he chuckled.

Irina laughed. 'Yes, it was one thing about our country I also do not miss.'

Nikita gazed into her eyes. 'Is there anything you do miss?'

'I miss a good ballet.'

Nikita had to stop himself from revealing his surprise. 'Like the Bolshoi for instance?'

'I have never seen the Bolshoi. It is my dream. I did ballet lessons until I was ten years old.'

'Why did you give it up?'

Irina sighed. 'Sadly, my ballet teacher became very sick. She died of cancer two months later. As a child, I never understood why she could not just get better, but as I grew up and more people close to me became sick, I knew it was because of the state, and their lack of medication and ignorance from getting help from the West.' She suddenly became distant, remembering those who had suffered.

'That is very sad,' said Nikita, sympathetically.

'I noticed there is a production of The Nutcracker on at the Kennedy Center,' he said, changing the subject.

'I used to like the story as a little girl,' she replied. 'I remember a pop-up book I had, and I used to read it with my grandmother.'

The waiter brought their main courses. Nikita ordered another bottle of wine then waited for the waiter to withdraw. 'What are you doing tomorrow evening, Irina?'

'I have no plans.'

'That is good. Would you like to go somewhere with me tomorrow evening?'

'What do you have in mind, Nikita Yurisevich?'

Nikita gave her a crafty smile. 'I will leave it a surprise. But I know you will enjoy it very much.'

Following a dessert of Tiramisu accompanied by two cups of cappuccino, Nikita paid the bill and helped Irina with her coat. When they walked outside, they saw it was now heavily snowing.

'Looks like Moscow has come to America, at last,' he said. He caught her smile under her hat. Then pausing, drew her nearer to him for a kiss. They kissed passionately as the snowflakes draped them.

Across the road, Tutinev sat warm and cosy but bored in the car. He watched them attentively as he fiddled with the car radio. Every station just seemed to be punching out American rock and roll music. As a boy, he had enjoyed his violin lessons and studied the masterpieces of the classic Russian composers.

Irina huddled into Nikita's coat for warmth. 'Would you like to come back to my apartment? she asked. 'I have some Stoli.'

Nikita smirked. It had been a long time since he had the opportunity to taste real Russian vodka again. He gazed into her sea green eyes. 'Even if you didn't have Stoli, Irina, I would have said yes to your invitation.'

They kissed again as Irina shot a quick glance across the street at the embassy vehicle. She clasped her hand around his and pulled him through the snow. Tutinev turned the car around and followed them along Pennsylvania Avenue until they arrived back to the Foxhall Village area and to Irina's Soviet-owned apartment block. He stopped and pulled over across the street to watch the couple disappear through the double doors. The KGB minder then started up the car again and turned back onto the road.

UP Inside Irina's first floor apartment, Nikita had barely removed his snow battered overcoat when Irina reached down, kicked off her shoes, unclipped her hair and flung her arms around his neck. They kissed again, this time more passionately than ever. He ran a hand down her back and clutched one of her cheeks through her skirt. They were locked like this for a few moments until Irina backed away.

'I'll just go and get the Stoli.'

Nikita pulled her back. 'Let's forget the vodka, Irina. As much as I love Stoli, all I really want — is you.'

She looked at him, allowing him to pull her back. They kissed again, locking themselves into an entwining embrace against the door. Nikita then scooped her up into his arms and with her hair cascading like a black waterfall, he carried her to the bedroom.

The Plan

Early next morning, the KGB Rezidentura had his agent in his office for a debrief. Davinski looked across at Tutinev as he listened to his account. Afterwards he smiled to himself. 'Looks like there is romance blossoming at the embassy.'

Tutinev agreed. 'Do you still want me or Alexei to follow them tonight?'

Davinski paused to think this over, then shrugged. 'I think we can leave the lovers alone tonight. The comrade Ambassador thinks our surveillance might scare off the American, Jack Ramsey. Besides, it is good that Metzinov is now occupied with love. It means he is likely to spend less time with Ramsey.' Davinski climbed out of his chair and started to pace across the room, then halted to gaze out of the window. 'I am not comfortable with these meetings he has with him, Sergei. I have already approached the comrade ambassador, but he approves highly the two men should maintain their working relationship. We are looking at ways to compromise the American.

Tutinev gave him a smirk. 'Perhaps a night with Anastasia might help with this, I think.'

'Using a Swallow will be futile. According to Metzinov, Ramsey is happy in his marriage and is a family man. Sexual manipulation is out of the question. We will have to think of something else, perhaps using Metzinov to do this. I have ordered some special surveillance equipment from Moscow so that we will be able to soon monitor their conversations. I am most intrigued in what they actually talk about in the park. The device will fit neatly in your inside pocket. You will have an earpiece and there will be a mini tape recorder inside the unit.'

'Do you think Metzinov is disloyal to the Motherland, comrade General?'

Davinski turned to face him. 'In foreign lands, Sergei, even the most loyal of donkeys can be tempted by the freshest carrots. It is the very reason why a Rezidentura is made part of an embassy of the Motherland.

Tutinev nodded at his chief's analogy. 'Is he a risk, comrade General?'

'All diplomats are risks, Sergei. As we know from the traitors of the past, the temptations inside the chocolate box of the free West are an ongoing problem; we just have to ensure they keep their fingers out of it and their diplomatic leashes are not too loose.'

***

As Tutinev left Davinski's office, across the city, an alarm clock rang out on a bedside table.

Irina Statinova reached over the body of the sleeping Nikita Metzinov to deactivate it.

Nikita stirred as she kissed his bare shoulder. He flipped over and grabbed her waist.

'Good morning,' she said feeling him between her thighs.

'Good morning. What time is it?'

'It is six o'clock. We'll have to leave soon. I will make us some coffee.' She slid her naked body out of bed and pulled on a pink silk kimono from a hook on the back of the bedroom door.

Nikita dozed for a few moments to think about the night they had just had together. His feelings for her were now stronger than ever. He could not wait to see her face when he presented the ballet tickets.

She returned holding two mugs of coffee, handing one to him. She then climbed back into the bed and snuggled up next him. 'I really enjoyed last night.' she announced.

'I enjoyed it too,' he said, then kissed her fully on her lips.

She stared ahead at a print of the Moskva River on her wall. Nikita had the same print in his apartment. 'So, you said we are going somewhere tonight?'

Nikita nodded. 'I did.'

She tilted her head to face him. 'So, where are we going?' She gave him an inquisitive stare.

'As I said last night. It is a secret.'

She slapped him playfully on the chest. 'Nikita Yurisevich. You are teasing me.'

Nikita laughed. 'Don't worry. You will enjoy it, my love.' He began to caress her side, thinking how he had just addressed her. 'I promise,' he added.

They finished their coffee and after checking the time on her alarm clock, Irina rolled back on top of him, her face now inches away from his, and in one complete move, Nikita rolled her over onto her back.

Forty minutes later, they walked out of her apartment block and trudged through the few inches of snow which had fell overnight.

Later, at the embassy gates, they both showed their identity cards and nodded to the guard. After entering the building, they entered an empty lift. While it was ascending, Nikita moved to her, and they kissed again. The lift doors then opened, and Irina quickly adjusted herself, then walked out glancing back at him as the doors closed again.

At her desk, she removed her coat, sat down and thinking about him, gave out a satisfying sigh.

Nikita opened the door of his office then closed it behind him. Placing his overcoat on the back of his chair, he sat down and stared at the file containing the half-finished report on the B-1 deployment in Europe. He then began to think of Irina in her pink kimono this morning and how after making love again, they had enjoyed a shower together. He had then watched her get dressed, apply her makeup and brush her hair. He was looking forward to the ballet this evening. Perhaps he would then invite her back to *his* apartment. He glanced again at the file, then at the desk calendar. He had marked in the date for the Christmas party, the date which told him it was tomorrow night.

He opened the safe and pulled out the TU-160 technical manual. He had to take the photographs sometime today. He got up and walked over to a filing cabinet. Then, opening out the middle drawer, reached at the back to retrieve the miniature camera. He stood examining it for a few seconds then walked back to his desk and placed it into the pocket of his overcoat. This would be the most private place to keep it, he thought. He suddenly remembered the ballet tickets were also in the drawer of his desk and taking them out, he placed them into the inside pocket of his overcoat. The last thing he wanted was to forget them for this evening.

He turned to look out of the window. The light was good. A sunny sky had replaced the dismal dark sky of yesterday and from the Mount Alto location of the embassy, he noticed the snow covering the roofs of the other buildings was beginning to thaw - the temporary Christmas card image of the city had begun to fade away, although more snow had been forecast for today. He then started to think of a convenient time to take the photographs; it could not be this morning. The ambassador's attaché meeting was in an hour, and he had to complete the report by then. He could also hear other staff walking along the corridor. It would have to wait until after lunch. Everyone is more settled into their daily tasks, eager to get them finished before the end of the day.

His hands began to tremble with thoughts of his betrayal conflicting with his thoughts of Irina. In his mind's eye, he could see her face tomorrow night at the museum. The final glimpse of each other before he was smuggled out to his new life in America. He knew afterwards he would never see her again. Suddenly, the thoughts of Davinski looming over her as she sat at his desk trying to explain her innocence in his disappearance came rushing back to him.

The telephone on his desk buzzed. 'Metzinov.' It was Irina.

'Nikita. I have been instructed to inform you Ambassador Detrev needs to bring the attaché meeting forward. He wants to start at 8:30.'

He wanted to say something to her about last night but knew he had to keep things formal, especially when her communication would be open to others. 'Thank you, Irina.' He flicked off the internal intercom button. 'Damn!' he muttered, realising he would now have to take in the report in its unfinished state. There was barely enough time to make notes of his recommendations for monitoring the flight movements. The days of sending Aeroflot airliners with their distinctive transparent nose cones 'accidentally' off their projected courses into London were long over.

Nikita collated the documents he would need for the meeting and stepped out of the office.

Across the city, inside the National Museum of American History at the Smithsonian complex, Bob Donahue stood with Jack Ramsey inside a small room filled with cleaning supplies. Both held paper cups of black coffee. Ramsey had just been briefed on what was to happen. He still found it incredible that this was how they were going to get the Russian out.

'He should be safe in here,' said Donahue. 'I'll have one of my agents wait for him to leave the hall while Santa keeps everyone occupied. He will be taken back here by one of my men. For security reasons, the KGB agents won't have access, so they won't be able to reach him. When Santa finishes up, he'll be led back here then we'll lead our man out of those exit doors outside in the hall.'

Ramsey nodded his approval of the plan. 'I suppose he'll be taken to the Pentagon?'

Donahue shook his head. 'Actually, Jack, he won't be. We have a safe house north of the city. He'll be staying there for a while. He'll have to wear the hood in the car. It's also where we'll debrief him and do the polygraphs.

'And after that?'

'If he passes our tests, we'll take him to Andrews and fly him over to Edwards.' He'll stay on the base until we can decide where he'll be useful. That's where you'll come in. He knows you, and from what I've seen, he trusts you.'

'Do we have to watch anyone at the gala who could try and stop him? Donahue reached for his briefcase and pulled out a large brown envelope. He reached inside and placed three photographs on a table. 'This is Igor Davinski.'

Ramsey recognised the name. 'Isn't he the public relations attaché?'

'That's right. But what we also know is he's the embassy's Rezidentura. The head of the KGB in the US.' Donahue pointed to the other photographs. 'This is Sergei Tutinev. And this is Andrei Kirov.'

Ramsey nodded. 'I already know who they are. Those two goons follow him everywhere.'

'According to the diplomatic dossier we have, they're his secretary and his public liaison officer. Only these guys probably haven't picked a pen up in their lives. Intel received from Langley states they're both KGB thugs and serving a suspended sentence for human rights violations in Afghanistan. Davinski will have them watching their people like hawks. So, this is where we will also need your help, Jack. When the time comes, you're to grab our man and lead him as close to the door into the lobby as possible. Davinski knows you two are buddies so we're hoping he won't suspect anything if you get together and talk. When Santa arrives, all eyes should be on him, especially after the reception my wife will give him. You'll open the door and push Metzinov through to the agent waiting on the other side then just go back to the party. We'll take care of things from there.'

'Sounds like it'll work.'

'I'm counting on it.'

'And what about you. Where will you be in all this?'

Donahue smirked. 'Don't worry, Jack. I'll be there. You can be sure of that.'

Missing

Nikita finished his meeting with his ambassador and was now making his way to Davinski's office for his latest briefing to supply disinformation to Jack Ramsey. Although this was set for after the weekend, Nikita had to maintain the status quo.

As he walked along the corridor, he smiled to himself, thinking about Irina sitting next to Detrev as she had taken the minutes of the meeting. Now and again, she would make eye contact across the table and when there had also been an occasional, coy smile, he had tried his best not to show his feelings for her.

As usual on arrival, he found Davinski's door wide open, but he still knocked, out of courtesy.

Davinski flicked his head to him. 'Comrade Metzinov. Please come in. Some tea?'

'Please, comrade.' He watched as Davinski poured the tea into the two clear Russian tea glasses, then placed in the slices of lemon and passed one across the table to him.

Davinski looked down at a desk diary. 'Now, your last meeting with Jack Ramsey. I trust he accepted the information you gave him?'

Nikita nodded. 'Indeed, comrade.'

'Good. And what did he give you in exchange this time?'

Nikita had fully prepared his deceptive brief for the KGB. 'He gave me more on the B-1 deployments to England. He said that they will be evaluating their low-level capabilities through the Scottish hills at near transonic speeds. This will give the United States Air Force a complete report on their performance when they are used in Western Europe to strike at targets in the East.'

Davinski nodded his approval. 'This is most useful, comrade. What is your personal opinion of the B-1?'

'I think it is a most capable aircraft. I can see it will certainly be a future threat in NATO. The last administration cancelled the project in favour of the Minuteman missiles being deployed from their gigantic Galaxy transport aircraft but then the new war-mongering president took office and reinstated it to full production.

'Indeed, he did, comrade and I will be passing on your information to Moscow. When is your next meeting planned with Jack Ramsey?'

'Next Tuesday, comrade. At the International Arms conference in Texas.'

'Good. I will prepare some more rubbish for you to give to him. Maybe you can tell him that due to cuts in our military budget, we are going to reintroduce the Mig 17 into Europe,' joked Davinski.

Nikita laughed. 'I do not think that Ramsey is that naive, comrade.'

'Very well. I will meet with you on Monday to discuss our strategy.'

'Yes, comrade.'

Davinski leaned back in his chair. 'Comrade Tutinev informs me that you had dinner last night with Irina.'

'That is correct, comrade.'

'And that you went into her apartment, no?'

'We are good friends, comrade. I would not want to do anything to compromise her position.'

Davinski smiled. 'No, please do not take this the wrong way, comrade. It is good you and Irina are good friends. She is an attractive woman. I see nothing wrong with this.'

'It will not be reported?'

'Of course not, comrade. You will be with her at the gala tomorrow night?'

'Yes, comrade.'

'Excellent. I will be there also, and everyone will be watching everyone. It will be a counter surveillance circus; I am sure of it.'

Nikita chuckled. 'I think you may be right, comrade.'

Davinski grey eyes stared at him for a few moments. He then looked at his watch. 'I think that we can end this now. It is time for lunch.'

Nikita walked out of the Rezidentura's office pleased his meeting had gone well. The surveillance had been an advantage, especially with his actions with Irina at the park. The butterflies which had fluttered around in his stomach before the meeting, had now become hunger pains, and decided to head for the canteen for something to sustain them before returning to his office, and the traitorous act he was about to commit.

***

Nikita returned from lunch and discreetly checked outside his door, then walking back inside, closed it and walked back to his desk.

All through lunch with his colleagues in the canteen he wondered if Davinski had been cross examining him for reactions during their meeting, first with the conversation regarding Jack Ramsey, then with his comments concerning Irina. The last comment he made about the party and the emphasis on counter surveillance, had set alarm bells off in his head. Had this been a threat directly aimed at him? He sat down, opened the drawer and took out the technical manual for the TU-160, placing it on the table. He then switched on the desk lamp. It was a perfect light, everything on the pages would easily be captured.

Nikita smiled to himself. The Americans would get what they had asked him for. He reached into his deep overcoat pocket, his fingers searching for the small Minolta camera Bob Donahue had given him, but it was not there. His face suddenly went pale. He was sure he had not touched it since checking it earlier. He checked the other pocket, only to find the envelope with the two tickets to the ballet. After quickly checking the inside pocket, he began to panic. Then a sudden fear consumed him. *Did Davinski already suspect something, had secretly entered his office and found it?* If he did, he would have also checked the drawer to find the manual not secured in the safe as to embassy protocol. The camera and the unsecured manual on the Motherland's latest top-secret aircraft would easy draw the KGB man to only one conclusion.

Nikita left his office and slowly walked downstairs. In his mind he churned over again and again on what could have happened to the camera. If it was Davinski, then surely, he would have been called for by now and arrested under the flabbergasted eyes of the Ambassador. He knew one thing was for sure. With no opportunity to photograph the manual, and a possible threat to his life, and maybe Irina's as well, there was only one alternative — he had to steal it and get it out to the Americans. How he would achieve this, he had no idea. There was something else he had to think about, and that was how he was going to react the next time he saw Davinski? The man was relentless. His reputation as a successful spy catcher preceded him. It was the very reason he had been sent to be the KGB's Rezidentura in Washington DC in the first place — the protective king of a jungle where the fruits of freedom and betrayal resembled the capital's cherry blossom. When it had been announced Davinski was being sent to America, the staff at the embassy had suddenly begun to feel uneasy. Questions were raised. Fear of being mistakenly accused of being traitors to the Motherland had now made their excitable overseas deployment to the United States uncomfortable, and on his arrival, some had even decided to return to Moscow or requested a transfer to another embassy. Nikita had done the very thing that Davinski had been sent to suppress and he knew this loyal man to the Party and his two accomplices would be ruthless in their interrogation.

In the basement of the embassy, there was a small, solitary room. The room was empty barring two wooden chairs and a table. One side of the table had indented scratch marks in the wood, the other side had nicotine stains and embedded burn rings from mugs of hot coffee. Around the table, on the stone floor were splatters of dried bloodstains. There was one bright light bulb which hung down in the centre of this room. It was a room all the staff feared to enter, the room where the shouts and screams were muffled by the specially installed soundproofed walls. It was Igor Davinski's personal playroom — a room Nikita realised with the camera he had been given by the Americans now in the hands of the Rezidentura, might soon find himself being dragged across its threshold.

The Nutcracker

Irina had been waiting excitedly outside the embassy gates and her eyes lit up when she spied Nikita coming towards her. She smiled warmly thinking of the surprise. With meeting after meeting, and all the minute-taking she had been tasked, she had not seen him all day.

Nikita forced a smile in return.

She thought he looked troubled like something was worrying him. She reached up and kissed him. 'Is everything alright, Nikita Yuresevich?'

Nikita shrugged. 'Everything is fine, Irina, he tried his best to force the smile again. 'It's been a long day, that is all. I'm hungry. Let's go and eat.'

All through dinner, Irina was beside herself with what this surprise could be. She was also pleased to see that Nikita had returned to his usual self, making jokes and complimenting her on her choice of dessert. There was something else, but decided this could wait. The anticipation had been too much for her to bear. At this moment, she felt she was being teased by her lover. Bursting with curiosity, she yelled at him across the table. 'Nikita Yuresevich, you very bad man,' she said in Russian. 'Please, please tell me what this surprise is or I'll'—

Nikita laughed. 'Okay, okay. You win. I just wanted to see how long I could leave you waiting. Forgive me.'

Irina screwed up her napkin and threw it into his face; it landed in his empty dessert bowl. 'Now I forgive you,' she smiled.

'Good. because we are going somewhere very special. He reached into his pocket. 'It was not easy,' he slowly pulled out the tickets, 'but, I have managed to acquire these.'

Irina stared at the green booklet with an image of a traditional nutcracker on the front. Her mouth dropped open.

'Ona!' she shouted. Her Russian outburst had suddenly caused other patrons to glance across at them. She clasped her hands together over her face. 'How did you get these? All performances are sold out.'

'I have my contacts, Irina,' he replied. 'Shall we go?'

'They are for tonight's performance?'

Nikita nodded with a smile.

Irina jumped out of her chair alerting the waiter to fetch their coats from the coat rack. He then helped her with her coat. She thanked him, then quickly followed Nikita out of the door. Outside, she clutched his arm.

As they walked along the street, Nikita had suddenly relaxed about the whereabouts of the missing camera. Since noticing it was missing, he had not been able to concentrate for the rest of day. Every knock at the door, every buzz on the intercom and each time he had heard his name had brought a shiver of fear. He had expected to be summoned in front of the ambassador with Davinski and his men flanking him. But the call had not come. Surely, a discovery such as what was certainly a camera designed for only one purpose would have led to appropriate action being taken. It was very strange he was able to be here right now. He should be sitting at one side of the table in Davinski's playroom. But at this moment, he was walking with someone he realised he was beginning to develop deep feelings for. When they had left the restaurant, there was something else he had noticed. There had been no sign of Tutinev or Kirov. Why? Why had Davinski cancelled the usual surveillance for this evening? He began to further relax. Perhaps there was another explanation for the missing camera?

The Kennedy Theatre was beginning to fill with people taking to their seats for tonight's performance, and in the pit, the orchestra were warming up with a combined unharmonious wail of various musical instruments.

Irina noticed how elegant the women around her were dressed for this event. She gripped Nikita's hand. 'If I knew you were taking me here tonight, I would have gone home and put on a nice dress. Look at the other women - they all look so beautiful dressed in their evening gowns.' She looked down at her business suit to compare her appearance.

Nikita squeezed her hand. 'Do not worry, Irina. You look beautiful as you are. He lifted her hand and kissed it. 'I do hope you enjoy it.'

As she gazed into his eyes, the lights lowered. Then, and to the opening bars of the orchestra, the curtains parted for the start of Petyr Ilyich Tchaikovsky's masterpiece. They settled down as the orchestra started to play the first movement - a piece known as *The Miniature Overture.*

***

Later, inside Nikita's flat. Irina reclined on the sofa. She was still hearing Tchaikovsky's beautiful music in her head. The images of the colourful costumes soon followed as she relived the evening. Her host had gone into the kitchen to fetch hot drinks.

He returned to find her flicking through the programme brochure. 'You enjoyed the ballet, then Irina?'

'She looked up and smiled taking her cup of hot chocolate. 'Yes — very much. Thank you for such a lovely evening; it was a beautiful surprise. It also made me think of Ms Nadia my ballet teacher, teaching me my arabesque.'

'Who knows, had she survived and seen through your training, you could have been wearing one of those costumes tonight, on stage at the Bolshoi.'

She raised her mug. 'To my dear Ms Nadia- a wonderful teacher who finished her sessions long before her time.'

Nikita raised his mug. 'To Ms Nadia.'

She took a sip of her drink. 'What about you - did you enjoy it also?'

Nikita sat down beside her and shrugged. 'It was good. But Russian ballet dancers are better, I think. They are nimbler in their movements, even in costume. Though the orchestra were excellent.' His reply trailed off as the events of earlier in the day had gripped him again.

Irina noticed he had that far away stare he had when meeting her tonight. 'What is it, Nikita. You had the same look on your face earlier through dinner. Is everything alright?'

Nikita turned to her. 'We trust each other, yes?' He remained close in front of her staring into her eyes.

'Of course,' nodded Irina. She placed her hand on his. 'What is it, Nikita? Please, you can tell me.'

Nikita took in a breath. 'There is *something* I *need* to tell you.'

'Irina's face dropped. 'You are married?'

Nikita quickly shook his head. 'No, No. I am not married.'

'Then what is it? You are beginning to scare me.'

'I am in trouble, Irina. Very serious trouble. I don't know how to tell you this, but I am… going over to the Americans.' He looked her in the eye. 'I am going to claim political asylum in the United States.'

Irina's jaw dropped. 'You are serious? You are defecting to the West?'

Nikita just nodded.

She turned away, unsure of what she had just heard. Her eyes were fixed on a print of Moscow Square in wintertime - the snow caps covering the domes of St Basil's cathedral. 'I do not know what to say.' She turned back to him. 'When is this to happen?'

'Everything has been arranged for tomorrow night.'

Her eyes widened. 'At the Christmas Gala?'

Nikita just nodded again.

Irina's eyes blazed. 'How? How will this be possible? The Rezidentura? Davinski will be there.'

'The Americans are aware of this, Irina. They will know what to do. There is something else. I think Davinski is onto me.'

'What makes you so sure?'

The Americans want something in return - the technical manual for our new TU-160 aircraft. I have it. They gave me a special camera to take photographs of the pages. After my meeting with the comrade ambassador, I returned to my office and found it had been taken from my coat. I fear Davinski has it. I was expecting him to call me into his office today and arrest me, but this did not happen. The KGB could be coming for me at any moment.'

'And this is why you have been like this tonight?'

Nikita nodded. 'Yes. I am sorry. I fear you could also be in danger. Davinski may well assume you collaborated with me.'

'So, how long have you wanted this?'

'It was before we began to see each other, Irina. But now we are together, I don't know what to do.'

Irina put down her mug and walked over to the door. As she reached for her handbag, Nikita thought she was leaving. Their brief romance was over. Would she go straight to Davinski and expose him to save herself? She reached inside it and pulled out an object, and walking back, she stood over him and held out her hand. In the open palm was the Minolta miniature camera.

Nikita stared down in disbelief as if it were a nugget of gold.

'I was so excited to find out what you had planned for this evening that when I had to enter your office. I searched your coat — and found this. I did not know what to do, so I took it in panic and put it in my handbag. I was going to ask you about it. I thought Davinski had given it to you. But you seemed troubled tonight. Now I know why.' She angrily handed him the camera.

'Nikita stared down at it for a few seconds. 'So, no one else knows about this?'

She shook her head. 'I swear, Nikita Yuriesevich.'

Nikita sighed. 'Thank you, Irina. You have made me feel a little better knowing this.'

But. Doesn't change anything, you're still going to do this.' She sat down beside him and threw her arms around his neck. 'Please do not go to the Americans. I love you, Nikita. I do not know what I would do if you go.'

He kissed her. She had *also* used the *love* word. 'You could come with me. We could start a new life together, in America.'

She jolted back from him. 'I could not do that. My family are back home — they will be made to suffer - the stories you hear of what happens when someone defects to the West - the labour camps. I could not betray my family like that.'

Nikita kissed her again. 'I understand. But we will never see each other again. I do not think I could live like that, the thoughts of not seeing you again, ever, will drive me crazy. I have always been too busy in my work to find love, Irina. Now, I feel I have met the kindest and most beautiful woman in the world, and I am about to walk away from her. He placed his head in his hands and began to sob. 'I am now so confused, Irina.'

She leant over, pulled his hands away from his face and kissed him hard on the lips. 'Then let us not think about this anymore, tonight.' She stood up still holding his hand. 'There will be no more talk of this right now. We will talk about it in the morning. Tonight is just for us. Come, show me your bedroom.'

The Gift

Next morning they left Nikita's apartment. As Irina stepped onto the street, Nikita pulled her back.

'Irina, I think we should not go into the embassy together, this morning.'

She shot him a puzzled glance. He moved closer to her.

'It will be noticed if we arrive together. I think there are already rumours we are a couple. Nikita quickly looked around then lowered his voice. 'After what we talked about, we should be careful. I want to protect you, Irina.'

She reached up and kissed his cheek. 'I understand, my love.' She withdrew and walked alone towards the subway.

Nikita sighed. There it was again. He checked his watch. He would wait a few minutes so that he caught a later train.

At McPherson Square subway station, Nikita stepped off the train and walked up the platform to the exit. As he moved to ascend the steps, he was suddenly stopped in his tracks by a woman in her late forties with blonde hair. She held out an unlit cigarette.

'Excuse me, do you have a light?'

Nikita took a step back and smiled. 'Of course.' He took his lighter out of his coat and lit her cigarette.

She nodded her appreciation. Then looked closer at his lighter. 'That's a nice lighter. You must treasure it.' She looked him in the eye. 'I don't think you'll ever be without it, will you?'

He looked into her eyes in recognition to her comment. 'I try not to. I have only left it in my office once, I think.'

She moved closer to him. 'Bob sent me. Let's walk up the steps.'

Nikita walked beside her. Around them, the usual rush hour operated obliviously.

'You didn't show last night, as agreed. Bob got concerned. All I need to know is that you're still going through with it.'

Nikita remained silent. He had a decision to make and quickly.

'Well, what's your answer?' The FBI agent was growing impatient.

'Yes,' said Nikita, eventually.

She turned to him, looking him in the eye for confirmation.

'Please inform Mr Donahue that I still want to go through with it.'

She smiled. 'Nice to see you again,' she said raising her voice. 'Have a nice day.'

Nikita watched as she went ahead of him and marched over to a set of pay phones.

He arrived at his desk and placed his coat over the back of his chair, thinking about his strange liaison in the Metro. One thing was for sure, he was still important to them. At the Ambassador's meeting yesterday, he had volunteered for the task of preparing the Christmas gift for their American hosts of the framed set of Soviet postage stamps commemorating the successful link-up of the Apollo and Soyuz spacecraft in 1975. He had noticed how deep the frame was and how it could easily accommodate the manual.

Yesterday, Irina had delivered the wrapping paper shortly after the meeting while he was at lunch with his other attaché colleagues. There was a note saying she will be in his office later to do the wrapping. This must have been when she had most likely found the camera.

Placing the frame on his desk, he then turned to the safe and extracted the manual. He had been correct, the booklet fitted perfectly without protruding over the frame. Turning the frame over, he suddenly came up with a better idea. He used a letter opener to prise back the clips holding the backing board in place. Then, carefully lifting it out, he placed the technical manual behind the mount for the stamps, then replacing the backing board, he secured the clips.

He held up the frame, satisfied with his efforts. He placed it propped up under his desk. There would be no need for the risk to take photographs anymore. As far as his ambassador was concerned, the TU-160P manual would be filed away with the others in the archives. All he had to do now was get through the day and hope no one else would need it.

He looked at his watch. Irina would be at her desk by now. He had promised his ambassador his completed report on the B-1 deployment by lunchtime. Another thought had just occurred to him. The ambassador might want to browse about the TU-160 while reading the report. Had he concealed it too soon? With the report ready, he decided he would have it delivered by someone else, and flicking the button on his intercom, soon heard the soft voice of Irina.

'Irina. I have the report on the B-1 for the ambassador.' They both kept a formal tone during their communication although he wondered how she was dealing with her own conscience. following his revelation to her.

A few minutes later, there was a knock on his door, and she entered then quickly closed it. She ran over to his desk and fell into his arms.

'I have done nothing else but think of you since you left this morning, Nikita Yuresevich.'

'I have only thought of you too, Irina.' They kissed.

'Have you decided on what you will do tonight?' she asked him.

'I am still thinking about it, my dear Irina. I feel I must go. The Americans have prepared everything for me. He decided not to tell her what had happened at the Metro.

She looked around the room. 'And what about the manual for the TU-160?'

Nikita looked down at the frame of stamps. 'It is prepared.'

'She followed his eyes. It did not take her long to work out what he had done. 'You have put it with the stamps.'

Nikita nodded. 'It fit inside like a glove.'

Irina shook her head and tutted. 'You could just give them what they want. This way, we will still be together.'

'I am not sure, Irina. Right now, I do not want to leave you, but this is far bigger than just the both of us. If I decide not to go, I will still become a major asset to the Americans. The FBI will dangle me like a puppet on a string, and I will eventually be compromised.'

She bit her lip and turned to walk out of the office. 'I will see you later before the gala,' she said not looking at him.

Nikita turned to the door. 'Irina?'

She turned back. 'Yes, Nikita.'

'Thank you.'

'What for?'

'I think you already know what for.'

She nodded. 'I shall return to wrap the gift for you.' She closed the door behind her, leaving him with his haunting thoughts of the evening.

***

Donahue stubbed out his cigarette into the ashtray on Jack Ramsey's desk. 'I seriously thought we lost our boy, last night, Jack. And I also thought he'd maybe played us right from the go on this with that son of a bitch, Davinski.'

Ramsey sighed. 'But you managed to make contact this morning, or one of your agents did. And he's still A-OK for tonight. That's what matters.'

'Seems so. You remember what you have to do?'

Ramsey nodded. 'Just before eight o'clock, I lead him over to the doors, your wife addresses everyone, then when Santa appears, I push him through to your agent on the other side. I think I've got it.'

'That's it.'

'And you said you'll be there?'

'I'll definitely be there. You can be sure of that, buddy.'

'What if one of Davinski's men happen to be close when I lead him over?'

'Then it could get ugly.'

'What do ya mean, it could get ugly?'

'We're ready for anything. Those bastards even sniff what's going on, our agents will be ready to deal with it.'

'I don't follow you, buddy. Do you mean *they'll* be dealt with? Can you imagine the implications of taking out foreign agents on American soil and at a diplomatic event?'

'Relax. Hopefully, it won't come to that. Anyway, we wouldn't take them out, just give them a quick stab with something to render them to be sick. Everyone will just think they've had too much champagne. They'll just fall to the floor and throw up their guts. It will be enough to still get our boy out should it all go sideways.'

Ramsey shook his head. 'Jesus, Bob. You guys think of everything.'

Donahue lit another cigarette. 'We have to, Jack. It's called play-by-the-book, except when you come to a blank page.'

Ramsey nodded. 'There's still the problem that we haven't got the photographs of the manual. Metzinov promised me he would drop the film in the box last night.'

'He never went to the box. My guy followed him and the woman to the restaurant then they went to the ballet at the Kennedy.'

Ramsey suddenly did a double take. 'The woman?'

'Her name is Irina Statinova. She's Detrev's secretary. He's fallen in love, Jack.'

'Could this give us a problem? I mean is she gonna have to throw her guts up too, tonight?'

'That's why I sent my agent this morning. We needed to know he was still with us.

'Perhaps he's using her. Deflecting the KGB in some way.'

'You could be right. My guy reported there was also no sign of Tutinev or Kirov last night. Maybe, Davinski has called them off, leaving the lovers to themselves.'

Donahue realised what he had just said. 'Shoot. What if Statinova is working for him?'

'Do ya think that possible?'

'It would make sense why he didn't have a KGB tail last night.'

Ramsey smiled. 'Why send the beast when you could send Beauty to do a better job?'

Donahue suddenly displayed a worried look. 'We may be in trouble, Jack.'

'It's too late now. Our man is ready.' Ramsey looked at his watch. 'And in just over seven hours, it's all meant to happen.'

Here Comes Santa Claus

As the evening snow fell heavily on the Smithsonian institution's complex, the diplomatic cars began to pull up outside the National Museum of American History.

Nikita was in the limousine with his other diplomat colleagues following the one containing his ambassador, his wife and Irina Statinova. Behind him, another vehicle carried the embassy's Rezidentura.

Irina stepped out wearing a long green velvet evening dress, and with her black hair tightly up on her head, she almost outshined the wife of her ambassador. She caught Nikita's eye as he climbed out of the other limousine with his attaché colleagues. She also saw he was carrying the gift she had wrapped for their American hosts.

Walking inside, Nikita recognised Jack Ramsey and shook his hand.

'Nikita. Nice to see ya. Merry Christmas.' Ramsey looked down at the gift then looked back up at his Soviet counterpart. Nikita's fellow diplomats had already fanned out to be greeted by their opposite numbers.

Nikita gave a curt nod to Ramsey, the American instantly returning the gesture. Nikita then turned to his ambassador. 'This is ambassador Detrev and his wife, Katya.'

Ramsey shook their hands. 'Good evening, Ambassador, Mrs Detrev. Welcome to the Smithsonian.'

Nikita then turned to Irina. 'This is Irina, the ambassador's secretary.'

Ramsey gave her a cynical look then took her hand. 'Nice to meet you.'

They were suddenly interrupted by a tall woman wearing a glitzy sequin burgundy ball gown, her brunette hair clipped in a bouffant style.

Secretary of State, Gabriella Donahue addressed her Soviet guests with an inviting smile. 'Ambassador Detrev. It's lovely to see you here tonight. Mrs Detrev, it's very nice to see you again. She turned her attention to the entourage. 'On behalf of the American people, we welcome you to the National Museum of American History.'

Detrev shook her hand. 'Madame Secretary. It is an honour as always. May I say how lovely you look this evening.' He turned to his wife relieved to see that she had taken well his compliment.

He then turned to Nikita who handed him the wrapped gift. 'On behalf of the people of the Soviet Union, I present you with this gift. Merry Christmas, Madame Secretary.'

Nikita watched with anticipation as Detrev handed it over. He then glanced over at Irina who stared back at him with widened eyes. This was it. The drop had been made. He was now officially a spy and a traitor, and because Irina had wrapped the gift with full knowledge of what was hidden inside, she was now an accomplice.

Gabriella Donahue thanked Detrev then handed the gift to one of her aides. 'We will place it with the others under our wonderful Christmas tree. We also have something for you, but we have someone special arriving soon to give them out. In the meantime, please enjoy our museum and our hospitality and we will meet up again later.' She turned on her heel to greet more of the international arrivals.

Nikita observed the aide take the gift and place it with the others at the bottom of a dazzling twenty-foot Christmas tree.

Behind him, Igor Davinski moved forward flanked by Tutinev and Kirov in their evening suits. He scrutinised the scene in front of him, taking in the positions of his ambassador and his diplomats. He then noticed Ramsey approaching.

The American took Nikita's arm and pulled him over with him. 'I would like you to meet a couple of good colleagues of mine.'

As Ramsey led him across the hall, his ambassador watched gleefully as his military attaché once more was accepted into the American's circle.

Davinski gestured to Kirov to follow them.

Ramsey checked they were now alone, although Kirov was standing at a distance lighting a cigarette.

Ramsey had deliberately moved with Nikita near to the quartet of violinists. 'It's all set for eight o'clock. Santa will come through those doors and on his cry of Ho-Ho-Ho, you will make your way with me over to that door over there.'

Nikita followed the direction of Ramsey's gesture. 'I understand.'

Ramsey continued. 'On the other side will be an FBI agent. They'll take you to a room and lock the door. Don't worry, there's another key inside. You are only to acknowledge when you hear someone say - On Dasher, On Dancer, on Vixen.' Ramsey repeated the famous chant from the classic children's Christmas poem: *The Night Before Christmas.* 'You have the film on you?'

Nikita smiled. 'I have something better. The TU-160 manual is in the back of the frame, Ambassador Detrev has just given to your Madame Secretary.'

Ramsey had to stop himself from laughing out loud. 'I can't believe it. Wait till I tell, Bob.'

Nikita looked around the hall. 'I don't seem to see him anywhere. Is he here?'

'He said he would be.'

Over the other side of the hall, Irina was now standing alone, her ambassador and his wife had moved on to mingle with other ambassadors at the party. She saw that Nikita was with the man she had been introduced to earlier. She hoped Nikita would see her. She desperately needed to talk to him and decided to glide over to them.

Ramsey noticed her approaching them. 'I will let you get back to your colleagues. Remember what I said.' He moved away to join other colleagues from the Pentagon.

Nikita acknowledged Irina.

'I saw you go off with the American,' she said. I thought that was the last time I would see you. What is happening?'

'It is not time yet, Irina. Something is happening later for me to disappear from here.'

She clutched his arm. 'You are still going?' she said disappointedly.

He held her hand in his. 'The Americans have prepared for this. I cannot let them down. I shall miss you. We have had some good times together.'

She pulled her hand away. 'But that is it? You don't want us to be together?' She lashed out at his chest. 'If you must go, then go, Nikita Yurisevich! Good luck in America.' She turned and walked away from him leaving him dumbfounded and embarrassed. He had also hoped that nobody had overheard her outburst.

'Irina?' Nikita looked around the hall. Davinski was over the far side and was now watching him. He went after her. 'Irina. Please do not let us end like this. I have no choice. I have given the Americans the manual. I have betrayed the Motherland. If I stay, Davinski will arrest me and have me taken to the Lubyanka.'

'He does not need to know what you have done – what we have done' she added. 'This way, you will still be able to stay, yes?'

Nikita averted her harsh gaze. His eyes searched out Ramsey. What was he to do? She was desperate for him not to defect. Her eyes showed the sadness he had been dreading to see since disclosing his intentions to her.

'Do not forget, my love, I have also betrayed the Motherland by wrapping the gift.' she alliterated.

He turned back to her. 'I must go and speak with the Americans again.' He grabbed her hand kissed her forehead. 'I will see you soon, Irina. I promise. There is something I need to do.'

She watched as he brushed past her and walked over to a group of men sharing a joke. As he approached them, Ramsey gestured for him to join them and introduced him to the others.

Ten minutes later, the music had suddenly stopped to allow the US Secretary of State to make an announcement.

'Good evening, ladies and gentlemen,' greeted Gabriella Donahue. 'On behalf of the American people, I hope you are all having as wonderful an evening as I am. To welcome our friends from the Soviet Union, may I also say that despite all the difficulties we have seen over this past year with our two nations, it has been a privilege to honour Ambassador Detrev, his most charming wife and his staff in these celebrations. Some of you have made a special journey all the way from Moscow to be with us, tonight. In a few moments, we will be honouring another special guest. He's also travelled a long way to be with us tonight. But instead of travelling in the comfort of Aeroflot's Business Class, he has had to endure harsh winds, rain and let's not forget the snow, on a sleigh pulled by six flying reindeer named Dasher, Dancer, Donner, Blitzen, Cupid and Vixen. Ladies and gentlemen... I give you the one and only... Santa Claus.' She gestured to the doors, and as everybody turned their heads towards them, they opened to reveal a familiar, white-bearded figure in a red suit and black boots.

'Ho, ho, ho,' he shouted, holding out his arms, then carrying a large shiny red sack, stomped over to the Secretary.

'Welcome, Santa,' she greeted smiling into the face covered by cotton wool. Everybody clapped and cheered as she stood beside him.

Santa took the microphone. 'Ho Ho Ho. Good evening, everyone. It looks like you're all having a wonderful time,' he said, using a false Scandinavian accent. It was an accent this particular Santa had rehearsed for the past week with his wife.

Ramsey saw Nikita move towards him. He took hold of his arm and walked towards the back doors.

Nikita had finally managed to get away from being quizzed by Ramsey's acquaintances regarding his views on the Belenko affair and the FOXBAT aircraft. 'There is something I need to tell you.'

Ramsey knocked on the door. 'We're nearly out of time.' He looked over to see Kirov surveying the scene playing out next to the Christmas tree. He quickly pushed him through. 'Good luck. I'll see you in a few days.'

'But Jack?' Nikita's protest was met with silence as Ramsey closed the door.

Now on the other side of the doors, Nikita was met by the blonde female FBI agent he had met in the Metro. 'Well, hello again,' she smiled. 'Name's Joanna, by the way.

Nikita still distraught at what had just happened, decided this most probably was not her real name.

She guided him along the corridor to a grey door at the end, unlocked it, then ushered him inside. 'There's a key on the table. You need to keep this door locked until you hear the signal. I'll lock it now. Don't worry, you'll be safe. I'm just out here. Good luck.'

Nikita had not had time to take any of this in. It had all happened so fast. As the agent closed the door, he heard the click of the lock. He was now trapped - left alone with his own clash of thoughts - his thoughts of freedom, and his thoughts of Irina. When he had walked away from her, he had not even had the chance to say goodbye. He had seen the tears in your eyes, pleading with him not to defect. Now it was too late.

Out in the main exhibition hall, Davinski had found Tutinev and Kirov. 'I do not see Comrade Metzinov.'

'He was with the American, Ramsey, a few minutes ago,' said Kirov. 'Ramsey is over there.'

Davinski looked over at the group of Americans to see that Jack Ramsey was among them. 'Andrei. Check the restrooms. Sergei, come with me.'

Wanted

Irina was also looking for Nikita. She had to find him. She desperately wanted to try and talk him out of what he was about to do. She knew it all. Even after his confession of what he wanted the camera for, it still had remained a shock to her he would do such a thing. Right now, half of her wanted to be a good citizen to the Party and report him. Save herself, even though she had wrapped the gift knowing full well what was inside. If she did report him, she would leave out her involvement of passing the aircraft manual. But she feared Davinski would see through her; there would be the interrogations, the beatings, eventually she would confess all including her part in Nikita's defection. She would have no choice. She would then be on the next plane back to Russia. Her promising career in tatters.

She searched the scattered groups of people. There was no sign of him. Had he moved into one of the other galleries? She glided into a gallery where the Japanese ambassador and his wife were viewing Lincoln's top hat in a display case — it was the one he had worn to the theatre on the night he had been assassinated by John Wilkes Booth. They both turned and the man smiled at her. She surveyed the rest of the gallery — there was no one else in sight. She moved into another gallery to find a young couple being romantic with a sprig of mistletoe. She was frantically running out of options, and with no more rooms to explore, she felt the anxiety building within her.

Suddenly, Davinski appeared in front of her, stopping her in her tracks. Flanking him was Kirov. She tried her best to avert his glare. She could hear there were cheers and applause downstairs. It had then all gone silent again. The event with Santa was over.

Inside the storeroom, Nikita heard someone behind the door. There was also the sound of something being put on the floor. He listened carefully. There were three taps on the door. 'On Dasher, on Dancer, on Vixen.'

Nikita relaxed as he recognised the password. He carefully unlocked the door.

The man in the Santa suit stepped inside dragging the sack and quickly closed the door again. 'Okay, let's do this?' He stared at him through the white cotton wool beard and began to take off the red suit to reveal a tuxedo, white dress shirt and black bow tie underneath.

Nikita had not been told how he was to get out, but now it had become obvious to him - he was going to be leaving in the Santa suit! He smiled to himself, suddenly remembering what Ramsey had said about believing in Santa Claus.

The man took off the big black belt wrapped around his waist, then removed the jacket. Then after undoing the braces of the trousers, he pulled the cotton wool beard from his face. It was a face Nikita soon recognised.

'Hi Nikita.'

'Mr Donahue!' Nikita suddenly remembered his first name. 'Bob.'

Donahue's face then displayed a serious look. 'We haven't got much time. Your comrades in the KGB will be lookin' for ya. The car is waiting outside the front exit. All you have to do is stand at the doors and wave at the crowd.' The FBI man reached into the sack and extracted a pair of highly polished loafers. 'Time to get changed,' he said, removing his boots.

'I will ask you one more time, Irina,' asked Davinski in Russian. 'Where is Nikita Metzinov?' Even in her six-inch heels, Davinski towered over her.

She stood on the spot beginning to shake. 'I — I think he is talking with the American, Jack Ramsey, Comrade Davinski.'

The Rezidentura remained stern. 'I have just seen Jack Ramsey, Irina. Comrade Metzinov is not with him.' His eyes blazed at her. 'Tell me where he is, Irina!'

Irina started to tremble. 'I do not know, Comrade Davinski. I was also looking for him.'

Davinski shook his head. 'You know what the consequences could be for you if he has defected to the Americans, don't you, Irina?'

Irina nodded, forcefully.

'So why don't you tell me where he is,' persisted Davinski.

'I am telling you the truth, Comrade Davinski. I do not know. I swear on my loyalty to the Motherland.'

'You and Nikita Metzinov are lovers - are you not?'

'Yes. Comrade Davinski.' Then surely, he told you of his plans for tonight.'

Irina was tearful now. 'No. Comrade Davinski. Nikita did not tell me anything. You must believe me.'

Davinski remained standing over her, then eventually moved away. 'I suggest you go back to the party. There may be more questions I have for you.

Irina nodded through her tears. 'Yes, Comrade Davinski.'

He watched her as she turned and walked quickly back in the direction of the National Hall.

Approaching the hall, Irina heard the fanfare of party guests, but looking around, there was still no sign of her lover. She paused to survey her surroundings. Suddenly she was approached by her ambassador's wife.

'Is everything alright, Irina?'

Irina tried best to hide her tearful face. 'Yes, madam Detrev. All is well.'

'Where were you, you missed Santa Claus? He has gone now, through those doors.' She clutched her arm and smiled. 'Were you with comrade Metzinov, just now?'

Irina decided not to respond to her. She turned to the back of the hall. 'Please excuse me, madam.'

She walked over and opened one of them, now finding herself in a corridor. At the far end there was another door and through the glass panel she saw a blonde woman in a dark suit standing there with her arms in front of her as if she was on guard duty. A coiled wire entered her ear. Irina started to question this scene. *Why would she be here?* She crept closer to the door, keeping out of sight as she peered discreetly through the glass. Her answer soon emerged when the woman suddenly bounced to life on the appearance of Santa from one of the rooms. She walked up to him and escorted him towards the door leading back to the National Hall.

As soon as they had come through it, Irina blocked their path.

The tall, blonde FBI agent stepped in front of her. 'Please mam. If you could just step aside.'

Irina ignored her and stared over her shoulder at the Santa figure, taking in his height. In his right hand he gripped the sack. Amongst the gifts was the one she had wrapped containing the BLACKJACK manual. He stood looking at her.

'Mam, please step aside,' the agent repeated.

Irina gazed into the eyes half hidden by the white cotton wool beard. 'Nikita, please don't do this. I love you. Please stay so we can be together.'

The FBI agent had lost her patience. 'Mam, you need to move out of the way, right now.'

Irina stood transfixed at the man in the red suit. 'Please, Nikita. I beg you.'

The agent grabbed Irina's arm and pushed her out of the way causing her to become unbalanced. Irina crashed to the floor. 'I'm sorry, mam.'

They walked past her towards the main entrance. Irina lay on the floor sobbing.

At the front of the hall, Santa raised his white-gloved hand and gave the crowd a wave.

Irina quickly recovered herself from the floor and ran towards the front.

For a brief moment, Santa stood and stared at her, then flanked by Secret Service agents, he was ushered through to the outside and into an awaiting black SUV.

Irina watched the car move away then collapsed onto the floor.

A man moved up to help her and took her arm.

She looked up into the concerned face of Jack Ramsey.

'Are you okay, mam?

Irina shrugged him off her. She gave him a venomous stare then stood up and stomped away with tears smeared with makeup running down her cheeks.

At the side of the hall, she ran through a set of double doors and collapsed onto a bench and sobbed. She couldn't go back to the party, Davinski would be waiting for her. He had most probably seen her actions and guessed why. He would take his failure to prevent Metzinov's defection out on her. This time tomorrow she would be in the catacombs of Lubyanka prison, perhaps after a night of sleep deprivation inside Davinski's playroom. It all started to run through her head. The questioning would be brutal. What would follow, even more so. Betrayal of the Motherland carried the most severe of punishments. But it wouldn't be a quick process. They would leave her in solitude for a while, for months or even years, maybe use her as a stooge to spy on other prisoners in the communal cells, or even offer her a reprieve to have her train as a *swallow* honeytrap, finding herself being sent back here to lure an unsuspecting FBI agent in exchange for better treatment and improved accommodation. The thoughts of this made her recall the last ambassador, Viktor Miskiev, a crude, chauvinistic man she had found repulsive and how she would see the equally repulsive Anastasia Borodin breeze past her desk to see him. From behind the door, she would hear the laughter followed by other sounds from them of which at the time she did her best to ignore. There was even an occasion when she had entered his office to find him discreetly adjusting himself as the girl had quickly sat down on a chair at his desk. The thoughts of being forced to become one of these Russian dolls and controlled by Davinski, would be something she would find too difficult to bear.

Whatever her fate, she would answer for what she had done tonight. If they had also discovered what he had taken with him, then it might even just be a quick bullet. Right now, she wished she found the courage to have followed her secret Santa through the front doors to America. What had held her back she could not understand. Thinking about the evening's events again, she raised her knees to her face and buried herself in her dress.

A few minutes later, she felt a hand on her shoulder. Davinski had found her. She now wanted to bury her head forever.

'Irina?'

Through her trembling fear she heard the voice.

'Irina!'

It was not the voice of Davinski, Kirov or Tutinev.

'Irina?'

She looked up. Her eyes were deceiving her.

'I couldn't leave you,' said Nikita. He sat down beside her.

She glared at him, not quite believing it. She slapped him hard on his cheek then clutched his head and pulled him closer to her, kissing him furiously.

Behind them, the doors opened. Davinski burst through, then halted. He stood staring at the two lovers in their passionate embrace for a few seconds.

Irina opened her eyes and stared at him.

He nodded at her, then turned and walked back to the party. Irina clutched Nikita's hand. 'I don't understand. What happened?'

Nikita kissed her hand, then took out a packet of cigarettes, lit one then replaced the packet. 'Nothing, Irina. As far as tonight is concerned, nothing happened.'

'I was devastated. I thought it was you dressed as Santa Claus.'

'Believe it or not, Irina, this was to be the FBI's plan tonight.'

'So why did you not go through with it?'

Nikita turned to her and smirked. 'In the end, the Santa suit did not fit.'

They both burst into a nervous laugh then threw their arms around each other again.

Nominated for Best Thriller

2017 TCK On-Line Reader Awards

Wings of Death

An Alex Swan Mystery

1965, and the Cold War is hotting up. Dubbed by the press as the Silver Angel, the BR-101 Rapier, is the latest warplane prototype being produced for the Royal Air Force.

Controversy is already surrounding the project, as overrunning development costs and competition from an American rival and the British government are considering cancelling the Rapier.

At the plant, a young aircraft designer working on the Rapier has been killed under suspicious circumstances, and his fiancée wants answers.. With his colleague Arthur Gable, ex-MI5 officer, Alex Swan takes up an investigation learning a US-backed company are at the plant working on a new reconnaissance drone, called the *Python Hawk*.

Further incidents occur centred around the Rapier and key personnel are being mysteriously shadowed.

Swan and Gable are puzzled, suspecting a possible sabotage plot which they will soon discover links to a secret society dating back to the Revolutionary War. On their agenda, is murder, espionage and a plan to destroy the British aviation industry.

'*A Cold War Sherlock Holmes*' – *The Big Thrill magazine*

Available on Amazon Kindle and paperback.

About the Author

David lives in rural Kent in the UK and is married with three daughters. He is a former lecturer and writes study guides on selected texts for the English Literature curriculum.

He has written five novels in the *Alex Swan Mystery* series and the first book of a new crime thriller trilogy. He is currently working on his next Alex Swan novel and a World War 2 children's adventure.

David is also a member of the International Thriller Writers association and the Crime Writers Association.

His first book in this series, *Wings of Death*, was nominated for an on-line reader award for the Best Thriller category in 2017.

Printed in Great Britain
by Amazon